MORAL IMPERATIVE

8/19

DATE DUE

Help us Rate this book...
Put your initials on the
Left side and your rating
on the right side.
1 = Didn't care for
2 = It was O.K.
3 = It was great

Initials	Rating	AUG 2 6 2019 (MRH)	DEC 2 7 2019	JAN 0 9 2020	
MRH	1 2 (3)				
	1 2 3				
	1 2 3				
	1 2 3				
	1 2 3				
	1 2 3				
	1 2 3				
	1 2 3				
	1 2 3				
	1 2 3				
	1 2 3				
	1 2 3				
	1 2 3				
	1 2 3				
	1 2 3				

PRINTED IN U.S.A.

"MORAL IMPERATIVE"

GET A FREE COPY OF THE CORPS JUSTICE PREQUEL SHORT STORY, *GOD-SPEED*, JUST FOR SUBSCRIBING AT CG-COOPER.COM

Warning: This story is intended for mature audiences and contains profanity and violence.

Dedications
To my loyal group of Novels Live warriors, thanks for your help in crafting this novel.
To our amazing troops serving all over the world, thank you for your bravery and service.
Semper Fidelis

CORPS JUSTICE OATH BY COL. CALVIN STOKES, SR. (USMC, RET.)

1. We will protect and defend the Constitution of the United States.
2. We will protect the weak and punish the wicked.
3. When the laws of this nation hinder the completion of these duties, our moral compass will guide us to see the mission through.

* * *

Si Vis Pacem, Para Iustitiam: In order to have peace, you must first have justice.

MOSUL, IRAQ

12:15PM, AUGUST 8TH

Mikhail al-Mawsil could barely feel the beating. As his body involuntarily shook from the repeated stings of the lash, strikes from the rifle and kicks from a boot, his eyes remained glued to the altar in front of him. His senses seemed heightened. Focused.

Since he could remember, the Church of St. Thomas, one of the few Christian places of worship in his ancestral home, had been a safe haven. Even during the years of the revolution and the murderous round-ups of that tyrant Saddam Hussein, his people had flocked to the church. They were safe under the loving eyes of God.

Now it was defiled. It was a symbol he knew. The Islamic State of Iraq and the Levant (ISIS) had long wanted the city, and now they had it. Initially, it was thought that all the militants desired was control of the strategic Mosul Dam, but that was only the start. Soon they'd resorted to what had seemed to be random acts of terror. But al-Mawsil, who knew the face of such men from his days in the Iraqi security forces, knew this was a calculated act. A message.

His eyes remained locked on the altar where two boys sat. Eyes swollen from crying, the eldest of the two had his mouth split from where he'd been punched after defending his companion. They were his sons. His oldest, Yazen, had just turned twelve and wanted to be a soccer player when he grew up. The younger, Dalir, was only five, but he had a spirit much larger than his tiny frame. From the day he was born, the doctors said he would not live to see the next month, and yet, with the blessing of God, Dalir lived and thrived, chasing his older brother through the alleys of the city.

Without his wife, the two boys and God were all Mikhail had left. Somehow they'd made ends meet when the Americans left, and with God's help, his small family would never give up.

But now they had him. He'd heard of other Christians being captured, and he supposed they'd found out about him because of his background. His time serving his country once again haunting him, condemning him. He couldn't get away from it no matter how hard he tried. All he'd wanted was a country to be proud of, a land his children could grow old in. That's why he'd volunteered for service.

But it had not gone well after the Americans withdrew. Corruption ran rampant and the old ways soon seeped into his command. Cronyism and nepotism led to the outright dismissal of half of his unit. He'd left to care for his children.

He loved them deeply, and wished to spare them pain.

Again, the thump of a boot assailed his ribs, this time shaking his thoughts, probably cracking a rib.

"That is enough," came a voice from above.

He was panting now, trying to take what breaths he could. There was blood in his mouth, metallic and foreboding.

"End this now. We must go. Start with the children."

"Nooo!" cried Mikhail, receiving another kick in response.

Someone grabbed his hair and lifted his head. He looked straight at his boys as more men grabbed his sons and forced them onto their stomachs.

"Be brave, my sons! Be brave! God is with you!"

His finals words were drowned out by the firing of weapons, the bodies of his beautiful children bouncing from the blows. A cry came from the depths of his soul at the sight of his lifeless boys. Pure anguish. His heart broken. Never again would he chase Yazen across the soccer field and pretend he couldn't stop him. Never again would he tickle the ever giggling Dalir until he begged him to stop. Never again...

And then it was gone. A peace he hadn't felt since childhood flooded his body. He remembered it with stark clarity. It was when he'd almost died after falling down the well in his grandfather's village. He'd been down there for days. Freezing. Almost drowned. He knew what it was.

"Now you see what happens to heathens that deny the caliph," said the man standing above him. The others grunted their agreement.

Mikhail looked up at the man, his eyes bright with wonder, filled with tears. "God is the only One who may judge. Your judgment is coming."

Mikhail al-Maswil closed his eyes and never felt the bullet that entered his skull.

THE UNIVERSITY OF VIRGINIA

CHARLOTTESVILLE, VIRGINIA - 10:37AM, AUGUST 10TH

As was her right as Midshipman Battalion Commander, MIDN 1/C Diane Mayer sat in the front row of Maury Hall's auditorium. Sitting next to her were the Naval ROTC Commanding Officer and his entire staff. This wasn't a typical drill week, as school wasn't in session yet. What they were doing was prepping for Orientation Week, or O-Week as the student midshipmen called it. O-Week was the unit's mini boot camp for the incoming fourth class. Before they started the rigors of the University of Virginia, the incoming first years had to prove themselves to their NROTC peers and the unit staff. Anyone found wanting could have their scholarship pulled.

Most of the other meetings before had been about schedules and proper conduct. As the student CO of the unit, it was MIDN Mayer's job to ensure her staff was ready. There would be long hours, but the hope was that they could properly indoctrinate the future officers into their family.

The student and active duty staff was trying something

different this year. Instead of the usual lessons on leadership, they'd brought in a string of leaders who the CO, Captain Rollins (USN), had selected based on input from his subordinates. So far the leadership conference had gone off without a hitch. It had been an interesting collection of characters, most of whom had been to war and knew the perils of dysfunctional leaders. The practical lessons were relevant and well thought out.

But this last guy was different. Younger than the rest, probably in his mid-thirties, and much better looking than the old-timers before him, Cal Stokes kept MIDN Mayer's attention. It wasn't just that he was handsome; it was something in his eyes. A firm conviction that told her he knew exactly what he wanted and went after it with every ounce of his soul.

His demeanor was casual, yet formal. Wearing a pair of stylish faded jeans and a distressed sport coat over a black t-shirt, Stokes told them what he thought a good leader looked like. They were all things Mayer had heard before, but he said it in such a way that made the otherwise skeptical young woman an instant believer.

"You can't *try* to be a leader; you just have to do it. I'm sure you've heard it a million times: actions speak louder than words. Show your troops you're right there with them, that you'll give them everything you've got, and in time, you'll earn their trust," said Stokes.

Someone behind Mayer raised their hand. Normally this wasn't allowed in the middle of a talk, but Stokes had made it a point to tell them they should ask questions whenever they had them. Again, another small thing MIDN Mayer appreciated in an otherwise stringent group of males.

"Mr. Stokes, how do you know when you've earned their trust?" asked MIDN 3/C Gundry, one of Mayer's new squad leaders.

Stokes chuckled. "Well, it's not like they give you a badge or anything. You'll just know."

"Can you give us an example, sir?"

"Sure. Let's see. Oh, here's one. One of my best friends, a Marine officer and my former platoon commander, said he knew he'd earned at least a bit of his Marines' trust when he returned from a long night of setting up his perimeter defenses. Someone had set up his poncho, laid out his sleeping mat, and left him his favorite MRE, all without a word from him. He told me from that day on he could breathe a little easier. It sounds cheesy and simple, but it's the truth. Any other questions?"

Stokes had taken more questions than any guest speaker Mayer could remember. He'd answered honestly and without a hint of condescension.

The CO had passed the word, like he always did, to remain courteous and refrain from asking questions that could be considered controversial. They were still students, after all.

But MIDN Mayer had done a little digging on Calvin Stokes, Jr. and was prepared to use a touch of her well-earned capital to step into the gray area.

Mayer raised her hand. Stokes pointed at her.

"Sir, is it true that your cousin, Travis Haden, is the president's chief of staff?"

Stokes's eyes hardened for a split second, calming just as quickly. *I've got you*, she thought.

"He is," answered Stokes.

"And does that also make you a friend of President Brandon Zimmer?"

Stokes smiled. "I'd love to know where this line of questioning is going, Midshipman..."

"Mayer, sir. Midshipman Mayer."

"Midshipman Mayer, while I don't usually tell complete

strangers about my personal relationships, I think everyone in this room knows how to keep their mouths shut."

Mayer could feel the CO's eyes on her. She was sure to get an ass-chewing later.

"Yes, Miss Mayer. I am proud to say the president is a friend."

For a moment Mayer was surprised that he'd answered truthfully.

"Does anyone else have any—" Capt. Rollins started to ask.

Mayer spoke up again. "Mr. Stokes, if the president is a close friend, could you please tell us why he hasn't taken direct action against ISIS in Iraq?"

There was silence in the auditorium, and she was sure everyone was staring at her. She didn't care. What could they do to her?

"You don't have to answer that, Mr. Stokes," said the CO, obviously flustered.

Again, Stokes smiled. "It's fine. You remind me a lot of myself, Miss Mayer. Not afraid to ask the tough questions?"

She nodded her head, defiant.

"That's good. Just be careful. Every once in a while having a mouth like ours gets us bit in the ass."

Mayer flushed. She was sure he hadn't meant it the way it sounded, but she wondered what it would be like to have him...

"I'll tell you that I asked my close friend the same question. Not that I know what's going to happen, but here's what I will say. ISIS's time is coming."

* * *

THERE WAS A RECEPTION FOR THE GUEST SPEAKERS AFTER the leadership conference ended. Cal mingled with the midshipmen, genuinely surprised by their interest in him. He felt sorry for the retired admiral sitting in the corner, left alone by the student staff and trying to keep busy eating his slice of cake. He'd given a halfway decent talk, but something about his tone hadn't caught on with the audience.

Cal was just finishing with one kid when that girl, what was her name, Mayer, had the balls to step up and join the conversation. He'd seen the CO take her off to the side and give her a talking to. Apparently the aviator didn't like his flock straying off course.

Cal didn't care. It had surprised him. But what else was new?

"Midshipman Mayer, so nice of you to join us," said Cal, noticing the way some of the others rolled their eyes or looked the other way when she stepped up.

"Thank you, Mr. Stokes," said MIDN Mayer.

"Please, call me Cal."

"I'm not sure I should."

Cal shrugged. "What's on your mind, Mayer?"

"I'd like to apologize for what happened upstairs. I hope you don't think I was trying to put you on the spot."

"Oh?"

Some of the others laughed. Mayer's face stayed politely stern.

"It's just that..." She looked around, probably wanting to see if the CO was within earshot. "We don't get the chance to get to the heart of things sometimes. I hope you don't think I'm a total bitch."

The last word must've come out without thinking, because she covered her mouth as soon as she'd said it.

Cal laughed and looked at her. She had beautiful eyes. Blue with a hint of yellow. Her hair was pulled back in a military bun so he couldn't tell if her light brown hair was long or short. He swore he could smell her perfume, or was it her shampoo?

"Don't worry about it. I have a problem with keeping my mouth shut too."

Mayer blushed and they both smiled at each other.

Jeez. If I was only ten years younger.

CHARLOTTESVILLE, VIRGINIA

I t was two-dollar pitcher night at The Biltmore, and Diane Mayer needed it. She'd gotten a thorough ass-chewing from Capt. Rollins after the reception. Maybe a couple drinks would lessen the sting.

That's why she was walking into the bar, alone. She wanted to be amongst the normal college students and forget about ROTC. It probably wasn't the smartest thing to do seeing as how PT was at 6am the next day, but Diane needed to blow off some steam. It had been a long day.

There were plenty of familiar faces that nodded to her or waved as she made her way upstairs. It was packed. Unusual for the summer. She wanted to go to the farthest bar and find a spot where she could drink and sulk.

Making her way around a clump of giggling sorority sisters, she bumped into a guy just taking a seat at the bar.

"Sorry," she murmured, still moving.

"Well, look who it is."

Diane turned, not really in the mood to be hit on from

some drunk meathead. She was prepared to give the guy her best disarming smile, the one that said thanks but no thanks, but that never happened. Standing in front of her with a mischievous grin on his face was Cal Stokes.

"Oh, hi," she managed to say.

"Oh hi to you too. Hey guys, this is the midshipman I was telling you about," he said to his friends.

One, a massive black guy with a perfect flat top, stepped up with an easy smile. "I've gotta shake the hand of the girl that made Cal Stokes speechless."

Diane shook his hand shyly, not really knowing what to say. She noticed Stokes giving his friend a dirty look.

"The name's Trent. Willy Trent."

"Diane Mayer, Mr. Trent."

"Please call me Willy. Cal you already know. This pint-sized Mexican is Gaucho," Diane shook hands with the short Latino who had an interesting dual strand of braided beard hanging off his chin, "and this guy over here is Daniel." Diane only got a soft smile and a nod from the guy with the blond ponytail.

"Mr. Stokes, I'd like to once again apologize for—"

"Are we back to the mister business? Come on. We're in civvies. Call me Cal."

Diane could feel her heart thumping faster. She wasn't used to being unnerved. "Can I buy you a drink as a peace offering...Cal?"

Cal's eyebrow rose. "Are you old enough?"

She almost turned on her heal and stomped off but resisted the urge. "I'm twenty-eight."

His faced scrunched in confusion. "Really? How'd that happen?" asked Cal.

"Easy. I was born and then I had twenty-eight birthdays." Diane smiled sweetly as Cal's friends lost it, Willy most of all, his bellowing laugh making half the room turn.

"Ask a stupid question, get a smart ass answer," said Willy, one hand slapping Cal on the back, knocking him into the bar.

To Diane's surprise, Cal colored. Was he angry or just embarrassed?

"Now I'm the one who's sorry. How about I buy you a drink, Miss Mayer?" asked Cal. Something in his brown eyes...

"My name's Diane."

Cal nodded and made room for her at the bar.

* * *

AT FIRST DIANE REMINDED CAL OF HIS NOW-DECEASED fiancée Jessica. But as they talked, the old memories faded a bit more. Whether it was the flow of alcohol or the company around him, Cal felt himself relax. It was the first time in a while.

Diane fit right in with Cal's friends. She wasn't afraid. Eventually he found out that she was the youngest of four children, the only girl. Her brothers had all served in the military, and surprisingly, so had she. That explained the age.

She'd spent five years in the Navy, but she was vague on what she'd done other than mounds of paperwork. Despite his initial reservations, Cal felt himself being drawn to her. There had been other girls since Jessica, but none that intrigued him the way Diane Mayer did. He liked to keep it casual. Too much work to do, and there was always the lingering pain of Jess's death.

Diane's intelligence was evident, and her self-confidence sealed the deal. Even though he tried not to, he kept stealing glances at her, often catching her doing the same. Part of him felt ashamed, like he was cheating on Jess. His friends didn't seem to care, and even the quiet Marine Sniper, Daniel Briggs, joined in on the conversation.

Before he knew it, Daniel announced that it was midnight and said he was heading out. Trent and Gaucho said their goodbyes too, Trent giving Diane a massive bear hug, lifting her off the ground, and then leaving with others.

They were sitting on barstools, their thighs touching, suddenly unable to talk. "I guess I better get going soon too. PT in the morning," said Diane, swirling her beer mug in circles on the wet bar.

"Yeah, I've gotta go out of town for a couple days."

Her hand found his and she looked into his eyes.

"I'm really glad I came out tonight, Cal."

"Me too."

* * *

CAL'S INTERNAL ALARM CLOCK TOLD HIM IT WAS 5:30AM. He moved his hand slowly off of Diane's hand and crept to the bathroom. By the time he came back, he was surprised, and more than a little disappointed, that she was up and getting dressed.

She smiled at him as she slipped on her shorts. "Good morning."

"Morning."

He felt like a kid again. He didn't know what to say. Diane didn't seem to have that problem. She didn't seem the least bit embarrassed.

"I've gotta head out, but I'll be done around eight. Do you have time to grab breakfast?" she asked, slipping on a pair of running shoes.

He admired her muscular legs and finally looked away, trying to remember where his shirt was.

"I'll be leaving town before that. Rain check?"

She looked disappointed, but then flashed him that beautiful smile. "You've got my number."

Pulling her hair back in a ponytail, she walked over and stood in front of him. Cal put his arms around her, kissing her softly at first, and then more urgently. It felt like she was melting against him.

She pulled back. "I really have to go. I'm in enough trouble as it is."

She gave him a peck on the cheek and ran out the door.

* * *

NO ONE SAID A WORD WHEN HE STROLLED BACK INTO THEIR new home on the corner of Rugby Road and Preston Avenue. Months earlier, after leaving Stokes Security International (SSI), the company his father had founded, Cal was tasked by the president to form a new entity that would continue the covert missions he'd conducted at SSI. It was just too much of a risk under the SSI name.

So Cal had chosen Charlottesville, Virginia, both for nostalgic reasons (Cal went to U.Va and SSI's second headquarters, Camp Cavalier was minutes away) and because of its close proximity to the nation's capital and the president. With the money and face of Jonas Layton, the tech billionaire the world knew as 'The Fortuneteller' for his prognosticative powers, Cal formed *The Jefferson Group*.

He'd brought along some of his SSI colleagues, including Marine Master Sergeant Willy Trent, former Delta operator Gaucho and Marine sniper Daniel "Snake Eyes" Briggs. Not only had Gaucho's 11-man team volunteered to come along, so had tech genius Neil Patel and former CIA interrogator Dr. Alvin Higgins.

Their cover was simple. Jonas was in high demand by companies around the world and owned multiple businesses to help him fulfill his clients' needs. The Jefferson Group would be a sort of hybrid consultancy on the surface, providing services to the federal government, corporations and friendly foreign powers. It gave The Jefferson Group's employees a cover to travel wherever they needed.

Away from the public eye they had a different mission altogether. The president had tasked Cal with rooting out threats before they became a problem. Simply put, Cal and the rest of The Jefferson Group team were the president's silent eyes and ears, accountable only to him. Highly secret and extremely deadly, the team had already notched several high profile takedowns, cementing their position in the president's back pocket.

"Have a good night?" asked MSgt Trent, who was in the process of pouring himself a cup of coffee from the commercial grade machine mounted to the tiled backsplash. Gaucho was sitting at the table with Daniel, each reading newspapers.

"Yeah," said Cal, going for his own cup of caffeine.

When it was obvious that Cal wasn't going to say anything else, Trent said, "For what it's worth, Cal, Diane seems like a great gal."

Cal nodded, not really knowing what to say. Part of him still felt guilty, almost like he was forsaking the memory of his dead fiancée. He changed the subject.

"What time are we leaving?"

"Whenever you're ready, boss," answered Gaucho, not taking his eyes from his paper.

"Good. I'll take a shower and we can get breakfast on the way."

Cal was looking forward to talking to the president. They had a lot to discuss.

EN ROUTE TO WASHINGTON, D.C

8:27AM, AUGUST 11TH

Cal stared out the window as Daniel drove. Gaucho and Trent were in the back laughing about something. They always were. He was supposed to be thinking about their meeting with the president, but he couldn't stop replaying his night with Diane.

He knew what the other guys thought, that he'd slept with her. Not that they would've thought less of him, but that's probably what they assumed. It wasn't that he hadn't wanted to, but something held him back. Instead of making the beast with two backs, they'd spent all night talking, except for the time it took for a quick hour nap. Okay, and maybe fooling around a little.

It was the first time he'd totally relaxed around a woman since Jess. Despite the periodic sessions with Dr. Higgins, Cal had found it very hard to loosen up. Sometimes he felt like he was wound up so tight he might snap from the strain. Not only had he lost his fiancée a couple years before, he'd also lost his parents on 9/11, he'd lost half of his team in Wyoming, he'd lost...so much.

Aside from his high operational tempo, loss was the only thing Cal knew. Luckily he had guys like Daniel and Trent around who'd kept him grounded and called him out when he was being too much of a hard ass. Life was tough enough. It was even harder when you were a bitter prick. He'd been guilty of it on more than one occasion.

He wondered if things could really change, if he could change. He sighed. Only time would tell.

* * *

THE WHITE HOUSE

The president was waiting in the Oval Office when they arrived. Travis Haden, Cal's cousin, was with him, as was Gen. McMillan, the Marine chairman of the joint chiefs. Outside of the president, McMillan was one of a handful of people who knew what Cal and his team did for a living.

Everyone said their hellos and took a seat. First, Cal gave the president an overview of the latest from Charlottesville and their ongoing operations. They'd been busy, but not too busy. Mostly they'd spent time getting established, following up on leads, and doing the odd guest appearance at the university.

"Good to hear you guys are settling in down there. From what Travis has told me, you've built a pretty nice bachelor pad. When do I get an invite?" asked the president.

Cal shrugged. "We've gotta take care of the boys, Mr. President." And they had. Between him and Jonas, they'd given the men the chance to take classes and finally enjoy some time to themselves. Most of them had been with SSI for years and had the battle scars to prove it. Even the hardest warriors needed a break sometimes.

Once the president was satisfied that things were going well with his newest covert project, he got down to business.

"I don't have much time, but I wanted to bring you all up to speed on how we're handling ISIS in Iraq. General, why don't you give them a quick rundown," said the president.

McMillan nodded. "As you've seen in the news, and I'm sure the president gave you a heads-up before, we're in the process of getting humanitarian aid to the Iraqis who've been displaced by ISIS. We've also conducted limited air strikes in support of Iraqi troops and Kurdish Peshmerga forces."

"What about boots on the ground, General?" asked Cal, glad that the U.S. was finally doing something, but realistic enough to know that it was far from what was needed. He'd been pestering the president since April, trying to get the authorization to do something to help, but Zimmer kept putting him off. He'd been reluctant to go back on his predecessor's promise of a full troop withdrawal, and he wanted to give the Iraqi government time to work out its own problems.

But the bickering in Baghdad hadn't stopped, and the violence escalated, now bolstered by a steady stream of ISIS recruits from across the region. ISIS wasn't going away and the Iraqis couldn't fend them off alone.

McMillan continued. "We've increased our troop strength at the embassy and we're going over proposals to send in advisors."

"How many people are you thinking?"

The president answered. "That's one of the things we wanted to talk to you about, Cal."

"Oh?"

"General McMillan has some friends he'd like you to meet."

"Can't you just tell me—"

"Trust me. Take a ride with the general and all your questions will be answered."

Cal didn't like suspense, even from the president, but he willed his temper away, hoping this might finally be the first step to taking down ISIS.

* * *

CAL WAS SURPRISED THEY WEREN'T DRIVING TOWARD THE Pentagon, assuming they'd go to McMillan's office. Soon they pulled up to a familiar gate. They were at the Marine Barracks at 8th and I, the home of the Marine Commandant and the Marine Corps Silent Drill Team. Cal suddenly remembered a random bit of knowledge from boot camp as the driver pulled up to the curb. The Corps' oldest post was founded by President Thomas Jefferson and the second Marine commandant, Lt. Col. Burrows.

How fitting that a group of former Marines now calling themselves The Jefferson Group was getting a chance to come home.

Gen. McMillan winked at Cal. "No safer place, right?"

Cal nodded. He hadn't spent much time at 8th and I. It wasn't really the place of a lowly staff sergeant to hang out at one of the most sacred places in all of the Marine Corps. He'd been to an Evening Parade with his dad, but hadn't stepped foot inside since.

They were ushered in quickly, snappy salutes all around, and a full bird colonel escorted them down the path to the perfectly manicured lawn where the Silent Drill Team put on their world-renowned performances. Some of the silent drill guys were practicing in a far corner, wearing PT gear and white gloves, rifles twirling in the air with ease. Cal had tried it once and almost cracked his head open with a spinning Garand.

"Are we going to meet the Commandant, General?" MSgt Trent asked, his eyes wide with wonder as he looked around. No Marine could step inside 8th and I without a little sense of awe. History oozed from the bricks and pavestones.

"The outgoing commandant has already moved his things out. General Winfield, his replacement, will be moving in soon. They're just letting us use the place for the day."

"Then who are we meeting?" asked Cal.

"You'll see."

They entered the home of the commandant and made their way to the dining room, nothing in disarray despite the change in leadership. There was a motley collection of characters mingling around the large polished wood table. They all turned as Gen. McMillan walked into the room. Interestingly enough, no one called, "Attention on deck."

McMillan motioned Cal forward and said, "Everyone, I'd like for you to meet the man who is not only a personal friend of mine, but also a close friend of the president. Gentlemen, this is Cal Stokes."

MOSUL, IRAQ

Hasan al-Mawsil crept into the chapel through a secret passage built by priests nearly a century before. It was used in times of war for shuttling parishioners in and out. He'd made the same journey many times over the years. His older brother Mikhail had shown him the hand hewn tunnel when they were only children, often using it in elaborate neighborhood games of hide and seek. He didn't want to think about the other times he'd used it. This was a new game. Life vs. death.

He'd been on the run for weeks. High on ISIS's target list, Hasan had barely escaped capture no fewer than a dozen times. Each occasion he'd escaped unscathed. There'd been help. The citizens of Iraq had learned how to survive under the veil of darkness, always aware. Mostly he attributed his continued luck to The Almighty, who'd seen his family through so much tragedy.

Today he moved tentatively, having heard rumors from friends. Dark words about darker deeds. The barbarians had taken his only brother and his two nephews as they'd walked to the market. More than a score of witnesses confirmed the tale.

Heart thrumming as he neared the small wooden door, Hasan reached out and pulled the simple iron handle. The smell hit him like a crashing wave, his stomach dropping. He now knew without a doubt what he would find.

After slipping in the hidden portal and closing it quietly behind him, Hasan stood and listened. He'd gotten used to waiting. Ambushes were common. His heart told him to move, but his heightened senses commanded him to stay. There were no sounds except for the incessant buzzing of flies. The last rays of daylight seeped in through cracked windows, illuminating the dust floating lazily through the musty church air. The place was a mess. Pews overturned. Someone had even taken a crap right next to where he stood statuesque.

Hasan closed his eyes and said a prayer before turning to the altar. *Father, give me the strength to do what I must.*

Slowly, with silent tears filling his eyes, Hasan walked toward the front of the sanctuary, ignoring the buzzing insects that were doing their best to dissuade his chosen path. Escorts of doom.

Ten feet from the steps leading up to the stone altar, the Iraqi fell to his knees, choking back the sobs that could give away his position. He had to be quiet, somehow contain his sorrow.

His family. His brother and two nephews. Mikhail and his beloved sons Yazen and Dalir. Once so full of life, so full of love. It had been his brother who'd taught him about Christianity and its all-inclusive reach. So unlike the religion of their ancestors and the anger of the new breed. The once lost Hasan had found the way. It was his brother's hand reaching out, but God who'd embraced him. A God of love.

Something in him knew his family's souls now resided in a better place, a place where death and pain could no longer touch them. Hasan took in the sight of his brother laying splayed on the stone crafted altar, his two sons stacked on top of him, similarly lain, an enormous scimitar skewering the three together like some macabre kabob.

Not without effort, the last remaining al-Mawsil stood and walked to the unholy display. Repeating a prayer over and over for strength, he reached up and pulled the bloodied sword from the bodies of his loved ones, Dalir shifting precariously as the blade unsettled his body.

Hasan dropped the scimitar and caught Dalir's tiny body just before it slipped to the floor, his clouded dead eyes looking up at his uncle as he fell. Something gave Hasan the strength to endure. He knew there was much to do, but first he had to lay his family to rest.

It took him over two exhausting hours to drag the three bodies out of the concealed tunnel and into the waiting hands of his friends, fellow Christians.

They would be buried that night, sent to paradise aloft wings of love.

Tomorrow, Hasan would get to work.

* * *

NOT A MILE AWAY, THE ENEMY FORCE PREPPED FOR THE night, guards surrounding the two square blocks of homes they'd captured days before. Fire blazed to augment the intermittent street lights. Anyone moving through the captured portion of the city without a member of the Islamic state stood a good chance of being shot on sight.

"We've dispatched seventy-two of ninety-one agitators on the list, Commander."

The ISIS commander grunted, not looking up from his

laptop. His long fingers moved swiftly across the keyboard. He was in the middle of posting another magnificent beheading on their social media accounts. Oh, what they would have been able to do in the 1990s if they'd had the same technology. The world's media did his job for him, spreading the updates like wildfire.

How fitting that the very invention developed by the western devils now allowed his people to spread the Islamic caliphate's blessed word. Their deeds struck fear into the spoiled heathens and inflamed the passion of true believers.

They called him The Master and home was wherever the road took him. No one knew his real name. Truth be told, he hardly remembered it himself.

He'd trained in Syria and Gaza. He'd killed his first man in Iran on a raid in the late nineties, just a young man at the time. Since then he'd risen in the eyes of his men, justly earning command of a large portion of ISIS's growing army. That was one of their strengths. Command was born not of nepotism, but of skill and experience. The best man for the job.

Not merely a brute who used force indiscriminately, The Master was cunning, first studying his targets. Where his peers were happy to travel in caravans killing at will, The Master saw the weakness in such tactics. They had to curry the favor of the people through a careful combination of fear and acceptance if their new empire was to be ruled.

It was inevitable that certain elements would have to be eliminated, but The Master understood that unlike the old days, ISIS could not simply rape and pillage. They did not have a logistics train that could supply them on the move. It was necessary to live off the land, taking what they needed as they traveled. A well destroyed was no longer a well.

The Master had killed every man in one of his particularly overzealous units. Instead of following his orders, the band had terrorized a key community of government leaders known for its ability to flip sides as the tides turned. The Master saw the officials as a vital part of controlling the town, but they'd been paraded through the streets before being shot and thrown into an open air pit.

The lesson relayed, the guilty party's heads now sat atop spikes mounted to his vehicle. No other incidents had occurred without The Master's specific direction. His word was final.

"Have you found the priests yet?" asked The Master.

"Only one, commander," said the underling, his head bowed in deference.

"Find the others and bring them to me."

The captain knew he was being dismissed and left the compound without another word. There was much to do.

The Master stood and walked to a map tacked to the wall, portions colored in as they'd moved through their new kingdom. He reached out with a finger and slowly traced a line around the city of Mosul.

CHARLOTTESVILLE, VIRGINIA

10:20PM, AUGUST 11TH

The fire crackled in the stone fire pit, every once in a while letting off a soft hiss from a piece of still wet wood. Bass thumped in the distance, the nearest fraternities mere blocks away. The parties were just getting started, the murmur of students passing by on their way to the beer taps.

Cal heard none of it. He'd been nursing the same drink for over an hour. He had a lot to think about. Everyone else was either in bed or almost there.

The president and Gen. McMillan had really thrown him a curve ball. His four months of prodding had worked. He couldn't believe it. He'd asked for it.

Thinking back to the meeting in the Commandant's home earlier that day, he wondered how it would all pan out.

AFTER INTRODUCING HIM TO THE ROOM, GEN. MCMILLAN explained what was going to happen.

"First, thank you all for coming. You wouldn't be here if

you hadn't come on the personal invitation of President Zimmer through your countries' leaders. Now, let's talk about the situation. The Islamists of ISIS, ISIL, IS, whatever we're calling them these days, they're swallowing up vast portions of Iraq and any material they can find. You've seen the videos. Some of you have even been on the ground. Coerced religious conversion. Plunder. Mass murder.

"The bad news is that most world leaders are reluctant to return conventional troops to the region. Hell, *we* were the ones spearheading the draw-down." The disgusted look on McMillan's face showed the room what he really felt about the blanket withdrawal from the Middle East.

"The good news is that some of us believe it's time to put away the white gloves and come out swinging. ISIS thinks we won't answer. That leaves us with the men in this room. Except for yours truly, the rest of you are private citizens, civilian security contractors, military veterans. You received this invitation because it's time to join efforts, to combine our talents."

Cal had looked around the room. There were nods from most. Stern men. Serious operators. The first thing he'd thought when walking into the room was that he was being inducted into some secret warrior society.

McMillan continued. "You've answered the call, and for that you have my thanks. As you may have noticed, you each brought three representatives from your respective countries. President Zimmer and I have been working for months on forming this unofficial coalition. Publicly, none of this exists. If captured, you're on your own. Unofficially, we'll do everything we can to provide you with support, and get you out if the need arises. You'll be supplied with a list of supporting arms and close air assets, much of it coming from our carrier group in the Persian Gulf. That being said, let me introduce the respective leaders in the room."

In total, there were five groups, each comprised of three men. Five countries had come to the president's call.

The first two groups Cal expected.

The British contingent was led by Gene Kreyling, a former SAS operator with his left eye patched. He only nodded when introduced.

The Aussie team leader's name was Owen Fox, a tall freckle-faced man with a mischievous smile. He looked more surfer than operator, but was apparently a former Australian commando. Cal liked him immediately.

To Cal's surprise there was a Japanese contingent led by a wiry guy by the name of Takumi Kokubu. His English was perfect, if a bit clipped, and his mannerisms were proper, like many of the Japanese Cal had met over the years.

Another revelation, the Bulgarians, were introduced next, the gruffest of the bunch. Their chief, Stojan Valko, stood at ramrod attention as he was introduced, leveling a wary glare at Cal.

The Italians were led by a man with a cocky grin who bowed to the crowd as if wooing a pretty woman. He looked like he might've been more at home giving roses to passing female tourists on the Spanish Steps in Rome. His name was Stefano Moretti, and he reminded Cal of one of those fancy Italian actors who was always sweeping foreign women off their feet in movies. "A pleasure to meet you all," he'd said eloquently.

"There will be time for you to get to know each other soon," said McMillan. "Are there any questions for me?"

Cal had been the one to ask the obvious question. "General, I'm sure everyone's wondering, who's leading our merry band off to war?"

McMillian answered with a look of amusement. "I'm surprised you hadn't put it together, Cal, seeing as how you've been the one bugging the president about...how did you put it? *Getting his hippie ass up and doing something?*"

There were chuckles from the Aussies and Italians. Cal shrugged. "He asked my opinion, General." It was the truth. Cal had heard enough of the hemming and hawing. Something had to be done about ISIS.

McMillan looked to the others. "In case you hadn't figured it out, gentlemen, Cal Stokes will once and always be a United States Marine. Hard to get us knuckle draggers to keep our mouths shut, isn't it, Cal?"

Cal had grinned. "Yes, sir."

"Let me make it official. Cal will lead the American contingent and will be the de facto leader of this merry band of warriors, as Cal so eloquently put it. Anything you need goes through him."

Cal could tell by the looks on their faces that the others weren't happy with the decision. These men were leaders, their countenance said as much. The only people they were used to taking orders from were their own governments.

"Are there any other questions, gentlemen?" MacMillan asked.

There were none. Everyone was digesting the news, most leery of the new alliance. It was natural. Cal knew how he would've felt had he been in their shoes, but he wasn't. None of the others could deny that the United States had the best chance of turning the tide. It might take time, but Cal knew he'd prove to them the decision was based on merit, something any good warrior understood. The best man for the job.

CAL SWALLOWED HIS LAST SIP OF SCOTCH AS HE WALKED into the house. He needed sleep. *My ass is dragging*. He had no idea when he'd get another chance to get a full night's rest.

MOSUL, IRAQ

1:28AM, AUGUST 12TH

He crept along swiftly, his movement marked only by the slightest sound. A muted shuffle or gravely crunch the only things left in his wake. Imperceptible to all but the keenest of ears.

There was gunfire in the distance, the repeated staccato of automatic weapons. The invaders. Extremist devils.

Hasan put the thought out of his mind. There would be time to think later. This was a night of mourning. No, not mourning. A celebration of life.

The outskirts of the city were the most dangerous. Less cover. More patrols. He had to be careful. A prayer escaped his lips as he moved. *Lord, guide me...*

It was a small unmarked cemetery. No tombstones. Only the close knit community knew about the sacred spot. It was ringed by boulders in sort of a half moon. Holy ground. The others were waiting, respectfully silent.

"Welcome, my son," said the priest, a short man who looked to be in his sixties, his beard pearl white in the soft glow of the moon. Hasan had known Father Paulos since his conversion to Christianity. It was the kind priest who'd baptized Hasan under the proud gaze of his brother.

"Thank you, Father," said Hasan, gladly accepting the loving embrace from the church leader.

"Come. All is prepared."

Hasan followed the priest, nodding to the others, four priests and a handful of fellow Christians. There was the youthful Father Yousef, who liked to play soccer in his flowing robes, often besting the neighborhood children with the glee of a toddler. Then there was old Hasem, the one-legged proprietor of a spice shop in the market. He'd lost his family long ago, another purge. He knew loss and looked upon Hasan with knowing eyes.

They'd already dug the holes and placed the wrapped bodies of his brother and nephews on a bed of lush green grass. Hasan could smell the fresh scent of the newly cut bedding. It reminded him of the days spent swimming and sunbathing with his family on the banks of the Tigris. Good days. Blessed days.

The others moved closer, hands settling on Hasan's shoulders and arms. A young boy's hand wrapped in his, an old woman's in the other. His people. Sharing in his grief.

Father Paulos began. "I remember the first time I met Mikhail. He told me a Christian priest shouldn't walk the streets..."

FIFTEEN MINUTES LATER, THE SERVICE WAS OVER. HASAN cast the first handful of dirt onto each of the three graves. The others did the rest, expertly filling the holes with practiced skill. There had been too many deaths over the years, too many graves.

Hasan watched as they worked. His tears were gone. His

family in his heart. They were close by. He could feel their presence. Mikhail's gnarled hands on his shoulder, Yazen smiling, holding a soccer ball under his arm. Sweet Dalir tugging his pants leg, trying to get his attention.

Hasan closed his eyes and smiled, savoring the feeling, thanking God for the vision. The images floated away into the darkness and he opened his eyes.

"What was that noise?" he whispered to Father Paulos.

Everyone froze. In his past life, Hasan al-Mawsil was a thief, a gifted street urchin surviving off of his skills as a pick-pocket and small time enforcer. His senses, honed from years of skirting the law, aided him now. The others knew to listen.

"Quick, get the others and go, Father," he said.

Father Paulos looked at him and then nodded to his fellow priests. Each produced an American-made assault rifle from under their robes, hanging from tactical slings. Hasan had never seen them armed before. It seemed so out of place.

"You take the others, Hasan. I will maintain the vigil," said Father Paulos, handling his weapon as if it were the most natural thing in the world.

"But, Father, they are dead and buried. Come with us. You are priests, not warriors. Let me stay," pleaded Hasan, not wanting his friend to sacrifice himself for the sake of the gravesite. The others were moving, gently urged by the other priests.

The fatherly head of the church smiled and placed his hand over Hasan's heart. "There is much love in you, my son. Remember to look to God when you doubt, when all looks lost. He will guide your hand. Listen to Him."

"Father—"

"Go. My brothers will be with you. There has been word from the Americans."

"The Americans?" Hasan asked, glancing over the priest's

shoulder. There was light in the distance. Muted shouts. The enemy was closing in.

"Yes. Now go, Hasan."

There wasn't an ounce of fear in his eyes, only the supreme confidence of a man who'd accepted his fate. Father Paulos turned, weapon in hand, and walked to meet the coming demons. Hasan said a prayer for the man who'd guided him to God. When others had said Hasan should be thrown out of the church, it was Father Paulos who'd defended him, taking him under his tutelage and showing him God's word. Always patient. Always loving.

Hasan took one last look at the priest's fading form, then turned and followed the others.

* * *

FATHER PAULOS WAS AN IRAQI BY BIRTH, BUT HE'D SEEN much of the world in his youth. Raised in a wealthy family, he'd lived as a playboy might. He'd rebelled and taken his riches for granted. It wasn't until his mother and father had been killed by a suicide bomber that he'd hit rock bottom. He sat for days in his London hotel room, drinking from an endless supply of room service liquor, his father's pistol cradled in his lap. Suicide seemed like the only answer.

On the third day of his binge there was a knock on the door. He'd answered it, surprised to find a young priest standing there with a piece of paper.

"I'm sorry, is this the Granger suite?" asked the priest in English.

"No," he'd moved to close the door, but the priest stopped it with an outstretched hand.

"I'm supposed to be performing the last rights for a gentlemen on this floor. You wouldn't know where I might find him, would you?"

"The Grangers live at the end of the hall," Paulos had slurred, again trying to shut the door. Still the priest held it.

"Are you well, son?" asked the priest, pushing into the room.

Paulos had stood there, wobbling, a pistol hanging in one hand. The priest wasn't shocked. He only nodded.

"Give me the gun."

For some reason he'd done as the priest had asked, handing the weapon over. The priest had set the pistol on a side table.

"Come. Help me usher Mr. Granger to the afterlife and then we will talk."

Again he listened, even allowing the priest to help him get cleaned up. They'd walked into the Granger suite and Paulos had watched as the priest blessed the dying man, a strange look of serenity lighting the old man's eyes.

Father Paulos remembered that look as he marched toward the approaching horde. He didn't hate them. He pitied them. But that would not keep him from protecting his flock.

Someone fired three warning shots not five feet from where he stepped. He kept walking.

"Stay where you are, priest," came the call, the word *priest* said like a vile curse.

Father Paulos felt the light fill him, his body tingled. He began to sing, lifting his weapon and firing a three round burst at his attackers. Then another. There were shouts and they returned fire.

A bullet hit him in the thigh, making the priest stumble. He willed the pain away, singing to God all the louder, joy blazing in his eyes. Something told him the others had gotten away safely. He could rest easy.

Suddenly the flare of a high powered light illuminated the lone priest, almost as if God was opening the gates of heaven.

Father Paulos knew what was coming but didn't flinch. He continued his song as the rounds ripped through his body, his life blood pouring from the fatal wounds. As he fell to the ground, the blackness swallowing him, he said a silent prayer for Hasan, that he finally listen to his heart and become a leader for his people.

CAMP CAVALIER

Cal watched as the Bulgarians moved through SSI's elaborate live fire range. They were good. A bit brutish for his taste, but still good. He doubted any of the three, and especially Stojan Valko, felt any pain. He'd probably give the giant MSgt Trent a run for his money.

Someone blew an air horn, marking the end of the allotted time. The range officer's voice came over the loud-speaker, "Cease fire! Cease fire!"

Cal made his way over to where the others were prepping. They'd started just after 7am, taking turns as teams of three. He'd gone through two times with Daniel and Gaucho, then once with Daniel and Trent. There'd been some grumbling about Cal's four man team, but Cal had ignored it. It was his operation and he knew there would be bitching regardless. A leader's job was to facilitate his commander's intent; in this case it was the president's intent.

Besides, both of his groupings were as fast if not faster than all but the Japanese. The unassuming Takumi Kokubu was a master of swift movement and pinpoint accuracy. Like a ninja. He'd risen more than a few steps in Cal's estimation. He wondered how the de-weaponized Post World War II Japanese had been able to train such elite warriors.

As he watched the Bulgarians exit the range, Cal noticed blood on Valko's face. It must've been from when the ballsy bastard ran headfirst through a locked plywood door.

"You okay?" Cal asked, motioning to his cheek.

Valko reached up and wiped his face with his hand. He licked some of the blood off of his fingers and walked past Cal without saying a word. Cal chuckled. There was always one hardhead in the bunch. As luck would have it, Cal had more than his share in the testosterone mix of alpha males.

The Brit, Gene Kreyling, had started it off. Despite the fact that Cal had deferred to the others on how they approached the range time, even letting opposing teams reset the configuration at will, the Brit couldn't help but complain about the arrangement.

"Not the way we do it back home," he'd grumbled.

Some of his bluster was lost when he watched Cal's first run through the path Kreyling had designed. Flawless.

As for the others, Cal was still undecided. They were all special ops trained and each team had their own style. The Aussies were like kids, reminding him of a bunch of caffeine bursting teens going through a paintball course. All smiles despite their deadly aim.

After an early lunch, they'd head over to the long range, each man getting the option to shoot from either 300, 500 or 1,000 yards. It would give Cal a better idea of how he could utilize the men. They had three days before hopping a flight first to Bahrain and then parts unknown. It wasn't much time.

He'd done a lot of reading since meeting the teams. Most people might look at what they were doing as suicide. A tiny force trying to defeat thousands.

Luckily he had access to a lot of classified after-action reports courtesy of Gen. McMillan. He and Daniel pored over the special ops accounts, marveling at how effective the small forces had been. He'd loved how the CIA's Special Activities Division (SAD) Paramilitary teams along with Army Special Forces had aided the Kurdish Peshmerga prior to the 2003 invasion of Iraq. Hell, they'd secured most of Northern Iraq!

Slowly, a picture developed in Cal's mind. Large ground forces had their uses, but it was the special operations forces who'd wreaked havoc on the enemy. Swift. Deadly. Invisible.

That's what they needed to be. Cal wanted ISIS to be looking over their shoulders, scared of shadows, hiding in rat holes. The approach had worked for centuries. Guerrilla tactics. Hit the enemy in unexpected ways. Always the threat of death raining down.

Yeah, thought Cal. *That's what we'll be. Shadows*.

* * *

THEY ATE LUNCH AT THE LODGE II, A REPLICA OF THE LOG cabin VIP quarters first built at SSI's headquarters, Camp Spartan, just outside Nashville, TN. Each team sat alone, still not mingling with the others.

"What do you guys think of the Bulgarians?" Cal asked his fellow Americans.

"That Valko is one crazy dude," said Trent. "Reminds me of those Greco-Roman wrestlers who lift people over their heads."

"You think you could take him, Top?" asked Gaucho.

Trent rolled his eyes and took a bite of his BLT.

"You think we're gonna have problems with him?" asked Cal.

"I think you'll have to be careful," said Daniel. "They're

good, but not as good as they think. What we're talking about doing takes finesse. You'll need to make sure they get that."

"Yeah. What about the others? Anything you've noticed?" Cal had his own opinions, but wanted his friends' take.

"I'm not sure about the Italians. Moretti's a nice guy, but they were the slowest on the range," said Trent.

"I talked to him. Seems they might have some other talents we can use," said Gaucho. "Moretti and his guys are bomb techs. I guess they did some work in Afghanistan for a while. He lost a cousin over there."

"That could come in handy. I should've thought about that. Maybe we'll head over to the explosives range if we have time. You know what, I've got an idea." Cal stood up. He couldn't believe he hadn't thought of it before. Stupid. Rule number one of leadership. Get to know your men. "Gentlemen, if I can get all your number ones over at the bar. Bring your lunch if you're still eating."

Cal ignored the annoyed looks and walked to the bar with the rest of his lunch. Instead of sitting at the bar, he went around the other side and stood at the bartender's station.

The five other leaders took seats on the bar stools.

"I wanted get a better idea of what we each bring to the table. Let's start with you, Moretti. I hear you guys are EOD."

Stefano Moretti smiled. "That is not entirely accurate."

"What do you mean?"

Again the smile, as if he was embarrassed to say. "You know the mafia, yes?"

Cal nodded.

"Well, my men and I are, what you might call, second-chancers. We were given the choice to go to jail or join the army."

That wasn't what Cal had expected. "You guys were bombers for the mob?"

Moretti shrugged. "I will admit we were young and stupid, but it is part of my country. Many of us do not have a choice. I had a certain gift for explosives and was recruited when I was thirteen. My hobby became my job."

Cal couldn't believe what he was hearing. McMillan had given him a bunch of mafia thugs? What the hell? "Tell me the story gets better."

"At the time we never targeted anyone except the soldiers of rival families. It was not until we were told to take down a mafia chief's house that everything changed. They told us the man was alone, but he wasn't. His wife, son and five grandchildren were there. They all died."

"And you got caught?"

Morretti shook his head, the first hint of sadness in his eyes. "I was twenty. I have always had a deep faith." The Italian pulled a gold crucifix out from under his shirt, making the sign of the cross. "After much prayer, I told my friends we had to go to the police. For some reason they agreed. They followed me to the Carabinieri station and we surrendered. We were at first beaten. I had my jaw broken. That night as we lay in our own blood, a priest visited. He was the priest who had baptized me. I had not seen him since I was a child, but he heard from friends that I was the one who had killed the mafia chief's family. He told me that God was not yet done with my soul. He said a prayer for us, and then left. The next day we were given the chance to go into the army. We went and I have been serving my penance ever since."

Cal didn't know what to say. Daniel would love that story. So Moretti had sinned, gotten a second chance, and then gone off to fight the extremists in Afghanistan. Interesting.

"So you know something about explosives then?" asked Cal, smiling this time.

Moretti returned the smile. "A little."

"What about you, Fox?"

Owen Fox grinned. "Snipers, mate. We like to shoot. The longer the better. Wish you hadn't asked, though. Me and the boys were planning on taking some of your money this afternoon."

"Kokubu-san?"

Takumi Kokubu nodded. "Medics. I was a doctor before joining the army."

Cal whistled. "And you ran through the range the way you did? I wish we had docs like you in America. Good to have you."

Kokubu nodded, a slight smile tugging at the corners of his mouth.

"Kreyling? What about you?"

"Urban assault. My team first worked together in Basra. Once Iraq settled down, we hit Afghanistan a few times."

"Valko, what about you guys?"

Valko looked back at him with contempt. "I am here to kill the Islamists before they can come to my country. I am not here to report to you, boy."

"I'd say that's out of line," said Kreyling, surprising Cal by speaking up. "Stokes is just trying to get a better idea of how we can all contribute."

"I tell you how I contribute. I kill. You tell me who, and I do it. Are we finished?"

Cal nodded and Valko stalked off.

"Don't worry about him," said Owen Fox, a smile still on his face. "He'll come around."

Cal wasn't sure. There was something he didn't like about the Bulgarian. "Let's finish up lunch and head out. Hey, Fox, you wanna make a little bet before we get to the range? My best against yours?"

"I'm game."

"Good. If we win you have to show me how to put a shrimp on the barbie."

Fox laughed. "First of all, in Australia we call them prawns. Second, if we win, you get to buy each of my boys a case of Tennessee whiskey."

"You're on."

AS HE WALKED AWAY FROM THE BAR, HE FELT LIKE SMALL part of the tension had lifted. He'd put the focus back on them. Let them look like rock stars. It's what every great leader did. Don't toot your own horn. Lead by example and give the credit to your men. If he could get four out of the five foreigners on the same page, he figured they had a good chance of coming home alive.

MOSUL, IRAQ

4:15PM AST, AUGUST 12TH

The preceding night and following morning had not gone as he would've liked. Not only were the Kurds being more resistant than they'd planned, the push to corral a band of nearly five hundred displaced Yazidis heading north ended in complete failure. He was exhausted, but there was still work to do before he could sleep.

Sipping from a ceramic mug of water, The Master waved his captain in. His underling looked nervous, his eyes downcast.

"Do you have the priests?" asked The Master, already knowing the answer.

"No, Commander. We were able to retrieve the body of one of the infidels."

"Where is it?"

"In the courtyard being prepared for your broadcast."

"Show me."

The Master rose and followed the captain out of the spacious home into the inner courtyard where the body of the Christian priest lay on the blood-soaked earth. The rest of his troops stood expectantly, their conversations stopped.

"I am disappointed," said the Master, walking over to the corpse. He couldn't make out the man's features so riddled was the body with bullets. But he knew the man's identity by his wardrobe. This was the man he'd longed to talk to, to make an example of to the world. Maybe that was still possible.

The captain fell to his knees. "My apologies, Master."

"Tell me how you misunderstood my instructions." The Master looked around the courtyard at the thirty odd troops standing with open deference. They too avoided his gaze.

"We found the cemetery and were closing in, but this priest," the captain pointed at Father Paulos's body, "he fired on our forces. There was nothing we could do but return fire."

The Master shook his head sadly. "The capture and execution of the heathen priests was to be a pillar in our conquest. Was I not clear on this point?"

The captain fell to the ground, prostrate. "You were very clear, My Master."

Again the shake of The Master's head.

"Have I not treated you all as my family? Never have I promoted a warrior who had not proved himself in battle. And this is how you repay my kindness. What shall we do? What shall we do?"

No one in the crowd said a word. They'd seen The Master's silent rage before and didn't want to provoke it.

The captain finally spoke. "Give me one more chance. I will find them, Master."

The Master walked over and helped the man up, even dusting off the front of his clothes as a mother might do with her child. The gesture made the captain relax, a hint of hope in his eyes.

"Come. Let us see what can be done to salvage the situation. The cameras are ready?" asked The Master.

The captain nodded, motioning for his troops to get the equipment in place. They moved to their task, arranging the lighting and video gear in the appointed places.

"Tie the body up there." The Master pointed to where he wanted it done. Men scrambled to do his bidding. "Do we have the calf's blood prepared?"

The captain's face went pale. "There was not time, Master. I can have one of the men—"

The Master patted the man on the arm. "That will not be necessary."

In the blink of an eye, The Master extracted a gold-plated long barreled revolver and shot the captain in the forehead, the back of his skull exploding, brain matter hitting the wall behind him.

"Quickly, drain the captain's blood and put it in two buckets," said The Master, re-holstering the pistol, his face calm. He left the courtyard and slipped out of the baking sun to make his own preparations.

THE JOB WAS DONE RAPIDLY, THE BODY OF THE unfortunate captain drained as the priest was strung up, arms and legs splayed.

Within an hour the set was ready. The Master exited the house and strolled into the courtyard. Now bathed and wearing a new set of combat gear, he had his golden revolver prominently displayed in a shoulder holster and a massive curved blade on his hip.

He had no need of a mask. The Master believed that those who concealed themselves for such tasks were cowards. Besides, he had the blessing of Allah. His faith was strong. No mask was needed.

He strode up to the priest's body. It looked like it was caught in some invisible spider's web. The Master pointed to the man behind the camera and nodded. The red light on the video camera came on and The Master began.

"My people. Today we celebrate the glorious death of one of our enemies, an infidel whose very presence in the city of Mosul was a curse on Allah's blessed name. For years his place of pagan worship was a stain on this holy land. It was only after this Christian demon murdered one of my own men that we were able to cut him down." The Master picked up one of the two white buckets laid on the ground and poured the blood over the priest's body.

"The blood of our dead will seal this devil's fate."

He set the bucket down and picked up the second one, holding it high.

"Let the blood of our lost brother bless me as I do what Allah has commanded."

There were murmurs from the crowd as The Master poured the second bucket of already congealing blood over his own head, the liquid drenching him like a horrid slime. After throwing the bucket to the side, he continued. Blood ran over his eyes, but he never flinched. He looked straight into the camera, eyes blazing.

"We have warned you. This will be the last time I repeat these words. Allah has commanded that you repent and come to the true Word. Any who join us will be forgiven. All who do not..."

The Master pulled the curved blade from its scabbard and turned to the body hanging in wait. Its edge razor sharp, the sword easily sliced through the cadaver's left leg with The Master's diagonal overhead cut. Then the right leg was severed cleanly, making the body sway back and forth, now only secured by the ropes tied to its arms.

With the ease of a master swordsman, he dismantled the

rest of the body piece by piece, the body falling to the ground after the second arm was gone just below the shoulder. He left the head for last. It only took one swing for him to sever it right through the red soaked beard. He grabbed the priest by the hair and lifted the decapitated head, turning to the camera.

He was slightly out of breath, but more than steady in his speech.

The Master looked directly at the camera, the deformed face of the head dangling from his hand and in a voice just loud enough to hear, he said, "Allahu, Akbar."

CHARLOTTESVILLE, VIRGINIA

The night air was heavy, the late summer humidity clinging to Diane's skin. She was the last one to leave Maury Hall, the rest of her staff having left hours earlier. The new midshipman would be arriving in a couple days and she wanted her people rested.

She'd rushed to get changed, having lost track of the time despite her excitement. Diane hadn't expected a call from Cal for at least a few days when they'd said goodbye at her apartment the morning before he'd mentioning being out of town for almost a week. Cal called to invite her to dinner.

Having had the time to think about their last conversation, Diane wondered what she could expect from the handsome Marine. There was something about him that she still hadn't figured out, something he was hiding. Maybe he was just reserved, not accustomed to sharing his feelings. He was a guy after all. She shook away the over-analyzation and looked at the time on her phone. They were supposed to be meeting at eight and she was still five minutes away. Diane picked up the pace.

* * *

THERE WERE ONLY A HANDFUL OF PATRONS IN THE ST. Maarten Cafe. St. Maarten's was more bar than cafe. Music played lazily overhead, concealing the muffled conversations of customers. That would change in a couple weeks when students returned, the buffalo wings and drink specials a popular draw. Pretty soon it would be standing room only.

Cal glanced at his watch. *8pm*. It was late for dinner, but he'd assumed correctly that Diane hadn't had time for a proper meal. He'd only eaten a quick breakfast and the lunch at The Lodge. He was famished.

The waiter was filling an order of wings. Cal's mouth watered as he smelled it coming out of the kitchen. He was about to grab the first piece of chicken when Diane walked in.

God she looks beautiful. She was wearing a flowing ivory tank top, and a pair of gray shorts, her legs accentuated by the cut of the shorts and the white wedge sandals. Diane had amazing calves.

She waved to him with a smile and walked over. He got up from the table and got a hug for the effort. They kissed chastely, Cal still not sure what was appropriate.

"I am so glad you ordered," said Diane, grabbing a wing as she sat down, biting into it hungrily.

Cal followed suit. They were halfway through their first order before either one spoke again.

"You look tired," said Diane.

He felt tired.

"It's been a long couple days. How about you? Everything ready for the boots?"

Diane nodded, grabbing another wing. "Did you meet our AMOI, Gunny Harrington?"

"Yeah."

"He's been drilling the hell out of us. I can't wait to see what he does with the new mids."

Cal chuckled. "I remember sweating my ass off on the parade deck at Parris Island. Hours and hours practicing an about-face. I don't miss that part of being in the Marine Corps."

"When did you enlist?"

"2001. Right after 9/11."

He'd been a student at U.Va at the time, less than a year from graduation. On 9/11 Travis had called and told him about his parents. They were killed in the airplane that crashed into the Pentagon. He'd later found the voicemail his dad left right before the collision. He still kept a copy in a safety deposit box in Nashville.

Not knowing where to turn, Cal first ran to the Naval ROTC building and begged to be sent to officer candidate school. The Marine Officer Instructor (MOI) informed him that he couldn't. He had to graduate before getting commissioned and that was only after he was accepted by the Marine Corps' highly selective officer program.

That left Cal with one option, enlist. He'd left for Parris Island less than a week later and never looked back.

Although he'd come to accept his decision, the loss of his parents still stung. He didn't want to talk about it.

"What about you? Why the Navy?" asked Cal.

"I wanted intel and they gave it to me."

"And you loved it so much you wanted to do another stint as a butter bar?"

Diane stuck her tongue out at him. "Very funny, smart ass. I know how enlisted guys feel about officers, remember? No, I knew my contribution in the ranks was limited where I was.

There's more that I want to do and being an officer can get me there."

"You're not trying to be G.I. Jane, are you?"

Diane laughed. "Are you kidding? I can probably give you a run for your money on the PT field, but I'm still a lady. I like to dress up. You boys can have your fun in the mud. It's not for me."

That's a relief, thought Cal. The last thing he wanted to discuss were the merits of women in combat. While he didn't necessarily deny there were a small percentage of females who could cut it, he still felt like it was an uphill battle. The Israelis had figured it out with their conventional forces, but they were in a different spot, surrounded by enemies. Besides, even the Israelis had only a few high level female operators.

The movies loved to glorify the hot chick assassin, tearing through terrorist ranks, a top model one second and a deadly killer the next. Cal hadn't met one and he was at the top of the covert game. He wouldn't tell Diane, but he was glad she wasn't out to be the next Wonder Woman.

They finished the first dozen wings and ordered another.

"What have you been up to?" Diane asked, taking a sip of his beer like they'd been together for ages. For some reason her familiarity made him smile.

"Oh, you know, work, work and more work."

"Anything you can tell me about?"

Cal shrugged. "It's pretty boring. Mostly going over reports and writing new ones. You're probably having more fun than I am."

By the look in her eyes, he could tell she knew he was stretching the truth. She didn't look pissed. He was glad. His work was one of the reasons he hadn't looked for a relationship after Jess died. There were too many questions, too many things he couldn't talk about. How do you tell your wife or girlfriend that you just killed a murderer who was about to annihilate millions? Sounds great in a novel, but it didn't work in the real world. Normal people, let alone significant others, couldn't understand.

Luckily, she changed the subject and they enjoyed the rest of their meal without the pressure of trying to impress each other.

What the hell am I getting myself into?

* * *

CAL WALKED DIANE BACK TO HER APARTMENT AND SAID goodnight. They kissed briefly. She'd asked him to stay, but he told him he still had work to do. Diane didn't pout. Another thing Cal liked about her. She took him in stride, not trying to sway him.

But she had done it without trying. He could feel it, the irresistible tug pulling him toward her. It was effortless, even though he wanted to resist. There were so many reasons he should break it off before it got too far, but he couldn't. He'd even prepared a farewell speech, practicing as he'd walked to the restaurant earlier.

That had all changed as soon as she'd strolled in. For a man who could charge into the maw of the enemy without flinching, the fact that he couldn't say no to this woman was, well, confusing. He wasn't going to ask Diane to marry him, but at least he felt like he'd finally found someone away from work he could connect with. Cal hadn't had a friend outside of the Marine Corps or his current station, other than Jessica, since college. That was a long time ago.

It was hard to relate to people in the real world after you'd gone through the things Cal and his men had endured. Tragedy and triumph. Death and glory.

How do you tell your neighbor what you do? *Yeah, man.*

Last week I flew to D.C., met with the president, flew to New York and killed a billionaire. Yeah, right.

As Cal made his way toward Rugby Road, his thoughts shifted back to earlier in the day. The rest of the training went well. While Owen Fox and his snipers were very good, it was still Daniel who won the day. The Marine sniper had so impressed the others that Fox offered to buy Daniel dinner, wanting to know all his secrets.

The Bulgarians were still keeping to themselves. Valko just didn't seem to care about being part of the team. He'd rebuffed Cal and the others at every turn. Cal was starting to think maybe Valko's team should pack up and go.

But that wouldn't work. Like it or not, the Bulgarians were part of the lineup. Cal just had to figure out a way to get them in line, possibly by force if need be.

As he turned right onto Rugby Road, he found a familiar figure leaning against a lamp post.

"I thought I had a tail," said Cal.

"Just doing my job," answered Daniel, falling in step with his friend. "How was dinner?"

"Do you even need to ask? I'll bet you know exactly how dinner was, down to what we ate and what beer we ordered." Cal was amused. Daniel had taken it as his life's mission to ensure Cal's safety. Cal could take care of himself, but having his lucky rabbit's foot nearby never hurt.

"Don't worry. I waited outside."

Cal shook his head. "How was dinner with the Aussies?"

"Good."

"Did you give them all of your sniper secrets?"

Daniel chuckled. "Just the good ones."

Cal had met a lot of marksmen over the years. Much like professional athletes, there were varying levels of skill even among snipers. Some were technically proficient. Others had natural skill, often bred from generations of family outdoorsmen.

Daniel was in his own league. He was the complete package, plus he had that intangible gift of the world's best athletes like Jordan, Woods and Ali. He'd heard others try to figure it out, dissecting Daniel's stance, his trigger pull, even his breathing. Cal knew it was much more than all those little things. Daniel Briggs was as much in tune with the world around them as the most cunning animal predator. He had a gift. He could sense a faraway change in wind direction, anticipate a target's random movement, and even the subtle shift in an enemy's tactics. Cal sometimes thought Daniel could see the future, so heightened were his senses.

There was no other man on Earth Cal would rather have by his side.

They talked as they made their way back home, going over the plans for the next day's training. Forty-eight hours left. There wasn't much time.

MOSUL, IRAQ

3:48AM AST, AUGUST 13TH

Hasan waited with the four priests. They'd told him to be patient, that their guests would arrive in time. Their approach would be cautious. He'd sat in the same spot for almost two hours. The priests tried to engage him in conversation, but he didn't want to talk. There was too much to think about.

He'd seen the video. Poor Father Paulos, strung up like a doll, doused with the Islamist's impure blood. While it enraged him, he knew without a doubt that the vile act wouldn't have any effect on the priest's soul, no matter what that monster said. The elder was in Heaven, of that fact Hasan had no doubt. He'd said a prayer in thanks for sparing Father Paulos any torture at the hands of the terrorists. Animals.

"They are here," said one of the priests. The four still had their weapons at the ready and Hasan was glad for that. He had yet to secure his own, something he would have to remedy soon.

Two men walked into the darkened room, faces obscured by cowls. They looked like common beggars or one of the many refugees who'd made their way through Mosul over the preceding months.

Neither removed their hoods until seated on the bare floor across from Hasan. Both men had roughly Arabic features, dark complexions, scraggly beards.

"You are Hasan al-Mawsil?" asked the first man, his Arabic flawless. He sounded like he was from the south.

Hasan nodded.

"I am Timothy and this is my associate Fazul."

"You are the Americans?"

"No. We are here on their behalf," said Timothy.

"Then who are you?"

"Would you believe me if I told you we were friends?"

"I'm not sure what to believe these days."

Timothy looked to the priests. One of them nodded.

"They tell me you can be trusted, Hasan. Is this true?" asked Timothy.

"It is."

"Then I will tell you where we are from, although that knowledge, should it be given to the enemy, would surely seal our fate, and possibly your own."

Hasan didn't know what the man was talking about. He looked like one of a thousand Arabs he'd met in his lifetime. What was the man getting at?

"You can trust me," said Hasan.

Timothy looked to his partner, who nodded just perceptibly.

"We call the lands beyond the Sea of Galilee our home."

Hasan's eyes went wide. "You're Israeli?" He couldn't believe it. Timothy was right. If the Islamic barbarians knew Jews were in Iraq, they'd drop everything to have them found, tortured and then killed.

"We are."

"Why are you telling me this?"

"So you know you can trust us, Hasan. We live in a world where loyalty swings in the wind, especially here."

"What is it that you know about the Americans? Are they coming?"

Timothy hesitated. "I don't mean to get your hopes up. This is merely a—"

"I risked my life coming here," hissed Hasan. "Now tell me what you want of me or be gone."

Timothy smiled. "The Americans need someone from Mosul. One who knows the area."

"Why? They know Mosul. Why do they want me?"

"You came highly recommended."

"From who?" Hasan couldn't believe one of his friends would divulge his name and where to find him. That sort of information was never shared with outsiders.

"It was Father Paulos."

The words hit Hasan like a sledgehammer. Why had the priest given the Jews his name? Of what use could he be?

"I don't understand. Why would he do that?" Hasan looked to the four priests questioningly. "Tell me why."

Father Yousef, the youngest of the four, answered. "Father Paulos believed God has a plan for you. It was in a dream that he saw you standing with the Americans."

What was going on? Jews? Visions? It was too much for Hasan to comprehend.

"I am a simple man. I have no skills," said Hasan.

"Not according to Father Paulos," said Timothy.

"What was it that he told you?"

Father Yousef spoke up again, his smile proud. "Who other than Hasan al-Mawsil knows the streets of Mosul better than the streets themselves?"

"But—"

"How many friends does Hasan have along the road to Duhok, Soran and even into the mountains along the northern border?"

"I—"

"Who better than Hasan knows the pain of loss and has the will to see God's people saved?" asked Father Yousef, his eyes gleaming.

Hasan didn't know how to respond. That wasn't how he saw himself. Yes, he knew Mosul and could probably walk it blindfolded. Yes, he'd spent years traveling the northern reaches of Iraq, making deliveries and the occasional side deal. But to say that he was God's instrument and that he was somehow worthy of such trust? It was beyond his ability to grasp.

"It sounds like your friends believe in you more than you believe in yourself, Hasan. Maybe you should listen to them," said Timothy.

His brother had often told him he had a higher calling, but Hasan had always assumed his brother was speaking of being a good Christian. The thought grew into a question.

"Did you know my brother?"

Timothy nodded. There was a hint of sadness in his tone. "I've known your brother for some time. We believe ISIS somehow found out about his involvement with our operations."

Hasan wanted to scream at them, to blame them for his brother death, for the deaths of Yazen and Dalir. But he knew that wasn't true. His brother was braver than any man Hasan had ever met. Where others ran from service, Mikhail embraced it, tried his best to better the country despite his younger brother's warnings. Instead of begging for money to support his family, Mikhail took odd jobs, never too proud to do honest labor. And his faith. Mikhail wore his religion with pride, never hiding it from strangers despite the risk of reprisal.

He imagined his brother looking on, smiling down at him, nodding his head, pushing him forward. *What did he know that I didn't?*

Hasan took a deep breath and looked at Timothy. "What do you need me to do?"

THE WHITE HOUSE

The head of Mossad didn't like coming to America. Maybe it was because of the cold reception he'd gotten from the last president. To make an ally wait over an hour while he finished his round of golf...

He had yet to meet President Zimmer, and had only come as a favor to the Israeli Prime Minister. Like it or not, Omer Reisner had a boss, and his boss wanted him in America.

He did not have to wait long. Five minutes before the prescribed time, President Brandon Zimmer walked into the Situation Room, two men in tow. Like anyone who knew anything about the United States, Reisner instantly recognized Gen. McMillan. The imposing Marine was hard to miss, as was his impressive array of ribbons.

The second man was much less familiar, and part of Reisner's assignment. Travis Haden was a relative unknown to Mossad. They known he'd served as a SEAL and was the former CEO of Stokes Security International, but his relationship to the president was still a big question mark. How had he risen from obscurity to the right hand of the throne?

Reisner hoped to get more clarity during his visit.

"Mr. Reisner, thank you so much for coming on such short notice," said Zimmer, coming around the table to shake hands with the Israeli.

"It is my pleasure, Mr. President," said Reisner, who was maybe four inches shorter than the handsome American. Reisner turned to McMillan. "It is an honor to meet you as well, General. I've heard that you are a man to be trusted, a man of honor."

"Thank you. I've always been impressed by Israeli hospitality," said McMillan, wrapping Reisner's hand in an iron grip. Why did Marines all feel like a handshake was some kind of a strength contest?

"I'm Travis Haden, Mr. Reisner," said the dirty blond chief of staff. Reisner could tell the muscular advisor was sizing him up, a sly grin accompanying his greeting. This man was confident in his abilities, but was definitely no politician. He had the look of a warrior, not a bureaucrat.

"Thank you Mr. Haden. And may I say, congratulations on the new position."

After coffee was served by a Filipino steward, the four men were left alone. Reisner figured it was better to let the Americans start, and busied himself with the cheese danish he'd picked from the mound in the center of the table. Sometimes the best assets an intelligence agent had were his two ears, and Reisner meant to use them.

Zimmer took a sip of his coffee and began. "I hope you don't mind that I've included General McMillan and Mr. Haden in our discussion. They are my two closest advisors and I value their opinions above all others."

That was good. "I will say, Mr. President, that it has not

escaped my government's notice that you have decided to align yourself with a Unites States Marine and a Navy SEAL."

"And I take it that you welcome the change?"

Reisner shrugged. "You know how we Israelis treasure our military."

Zimmer nodded. "Then we're starting off on the right foot. Good. I promise this won't be a waste of your time. First, I wanted to make this known to your leadership before I announce it publicly. I'm not in the habit of letting our staunchest allies find out my opinions second hand. To get right to it, I fully support your actions in Gaza and am prepared to give you whatever support is needed in the Middle East."

Reisner hadn't been expecting that. The Prime Minister would be thrilled to hear about the change. His country's relationship with Zimmer's predecessor was contentious at best, sometimes outright hostile. Reisner had understood the man's liberal agenda, but in a matter of years the president had squandered many opportunities and weakened American alliances with its oldest allies. The Israeli hoped Zimmer wasn't just *blowing smoke*, as the Americans liked to say.

"That is very good to hear, Mr. President. We would like nothing more than to be a most trusted ally."

"That brings me to my next dilemma, Iraq and the Islamic caliphate. I was hoping you could give us some indication of your intentions."

This was a slippery slope for the Israeli. He'd been directed to give the Americans just enough information. Sort of a test. They'd been stung before, losing long term assets who'd disappeared overnight. Reisner had the proof that the loose-lipped lackeys of the last president were the cause. He would not let that happen again. The veteran Mossad leader had to be careful, something he always strived to be, until it was time to pull out the battle axe.

"Like you, we believe the marauding ISIS forces pose a direct threat to security in the region, even abroad. The chance of severe destabilization in the Arab world seems inevitable should they be allowed to continue on their current path."

"Do you have assets on the ground?" asked Travis Haden.

Reisner knew the question was coming, but was surprised that it came from the SEAL and not the president. This man must hold significant sway with Zimmer. Reisner decided to throw them a bone.

"We do."

"Surveillance or action teams?" asked Haden after casting a glance at the president.

"I cannot tell you that," answered Reisner, seeing no need to give away all his secrets. Haden didn't press the point.

"What are you planning to do?" asked Zimmer.

"That all depends on you, Mr. President."

I'm not going to show my cards before I see yours, Mr. President.

President Zimmer looked at Gen. McMillan and nodded.

"Mr. Reisner, what I'm about to tell you is only known to a handful of people, and none other than the three men sitting in front of you know the full story." *Now we are getting somewhere.* "We are approximately forty-eight hours from inserting an American-led multi-national team into Iraq. It was our hope that your government could assist us in our efforts."

"When you say team, how large?"

"Nineteen men."

Reisner caught himself before coughing out a laugh. Nineteen men? What did the Americans think they could do with that? Didn't they know what they were dealing with? Tens of thousands of extremists willing to die for the glory of Allah. He'd told the prime minister that he was sure the Americans wanted to discuss direct action, but nineteen men?

"I am sorry, I do not mean to be rude, but I assumed you would do more than send nineteen men into the desert."

Instead of getting mad, McMillan smiled. "What I forgot to mention was that these nineteen men will have direct access to any weapons systems we have, including land based bombers, drones and our carrier group in the Persian Gulf."

Now they were getting somewhere. Fine. Maybe he should open the door a bit more.

Reisner looked to Zimmer. "Mr. President, I think we have something that could help."

* * *

REISNER WAS ON THE PHONE AS SOON AS HE REACHED THE Israeli embassy.

"How did it go?" asked his prime minister, a man who'd risen to his current post on a wave of bi-partisan support. There was not much he couldn't do.

"I will say I am cautiously optimistic," answered Reisner.

"Coming from you, that is an extreme vote of confidence, Omer. What did you promise them?"

"Nothing more than you and I discussed."

"Good. And their contribution?"

Reisner told him.

"Do you think that will be enough to stop ISIS?"

Reisner honestly didn't know. "General McMillan seemed to think so."

"And this Haden? What did he have to say?"

"He and the president are playing from the same sheet of music."

"And this is a good thing?" asked the prime minister.

"I believe so."

"Very well. Let me know how things progress."

"Yes, Prime Minister."

CHARLOTTESVILLE, VIRGINIA

Gene Kreyling adjusted his eyepatch and wiped away a bead of sweat. His boys were taking the lead. It was Stokes's call. Despite what normal soldiers complained about, Kreyling knew from painful experience that constant training, especially in urban environments, was a must.

Kreyling saw what Stokes was doing. After the initial evaluation, which the Brit hadn't been thrilled about but now understood, Stokes had moved on to mutually supporting maneuvers. Every team had to be familiar with the new gear they'd received and with the other groups. Luckily, the Americans were good teachers, and Stokes had a group of tech heads from SSI who were helping the operators work out the kinks. The last thing they needed was to go into Iraq with a shoddy kit.

"Rango, you ready?" he asked his number two, a jumpy git from South London. He looked like a squirrely bastard, but Kreyling knew no one better suited for the heat of battle. It had been Rango who dragged him out of a bullet-ridden building where Kreyling had lost his eye to an IED blast. He'd woken up in a hospital to Rango's grinning face.

"Right," answered Rango, bouncing from foot to foot like a soccer player getting ready for kickoff.

Kreyling looked behind him to the other teams just forming up. The Aussies were on some distant hill, ready to ping whatever targets the range master decided to pop.

"Pounder, this is Wahoo Six. We're ready," came Stokes's voice over his headset.

He'd had to ask the American what the hell a 'wahoo' was. It sounded like something a kid said when he got excited. Stokes had laughed and explained that it was the unofficial mascot of the University of Virginia students, apparently a fish that could drink twice its own weight. The hard drinking Brit, call sign Pounder for the way he bulled his way into situations, had almost laughed at the explanation. Almost. He wasn't that cozy with anyone but his own men.

"Roger, Wahoo. We're ready."

There was a pause. Kreyling tapped Rango on the shoulder.

The hushed order came a second later. "Go, go, go."

Rango turned into the concrete building, Kreyling and the rest of the teams right behind.

* * *

"First, I owe Fox a beer. The target operator told me about that shot you guys made. Impressive," said Cal, addressing the men who were standing in the shade, drinking water after the latest practice session. "Now for the bad news. Looks like we're still working out the kinks on comms. Do we need to run through it at half speed?"

Cal knew there was nothing wrong with the radios. They were Neil Patel's design. Highly durable and with extended range, even inside reinforced structures. The problem was the Bulgarians. They just didn't want to play by the rules. The latest incident involved Valko failing to let the team to his left know where he was, almost resulting in the Italians getting shot. Moretti was not happy and kept throwing looks at Valko. The Bulgarian ignored him.

"Okay, let's do it again," said Cal, grabbing his weapon and heading back into the sun. If the Bulgarians wanted to be stubborn, fine. But if they so much as flagged another team, Valko was going to get an earful.

Kreyling caught up to him. "Why don't you put Valko up front."

That surprised Cal. He'd assumed the Brit wanted the lead. "You sure?"

"It'll give my boys a break." Kreyling went to join his men and Cal kept walking. Cal appreciated Kreyling's suggestion. The Brit was trying to help.

Other than sheer brute force, Cal didn't know what the Bulgarians brought to the table. Sure, they were elite troops, but the fact that they didn't want to be part of the team made them a liability. *Let's see what happens when they're up front*, Cal thought.

When everyone had made their way back to the raid complex, Cal announced, "Let's change things up on this one. Valko, I want your team up front. Everyone else switch with the team behind you. Kreyling, you bring up the rear."

There were no complaints. Cal knew everyone but the Bulgarians were thinking the same thing as him: *What do we do with Valko?*

* * *

"At least they didn't kill anyone," said Trent, as he, Cal, Daniel and Gaucho sat in the air conditioned luxury suite SSI had loaned them at The Lodge. Cal had given the rest of the teams the afternoon off. They'd reconvene just after dark to do a night insertion.

"They didn't do bad, but jeez. They don't listen worth a damn," said Gaucho, taking a long drink from a Gatorade.

"I've commanded my share of knuckleheads, but this guy takes the cake," said Cal, now worried that he would have to drop the Bulgarians. What would that do to U.S.-Bulgaria relations? It would definitely piss off Brandon.

"Maybe you should talk to him," suggested Daniel.

"I already tried that."

"Try again?" said Daniel with that Zen master smile that had pushed Cal to do any number of uncomfortable things, like when he'd convinced Cal to talk to Dr. Higgins. Daniel was right, of course. It was his job as leader.

"Fine. No better time than now." Cal grunted as he rose on sore legs. "But you jokers owe me a bottle of Famous Grouse if it doesn't work."

THE OTHER BULGARIAN OPERATORS TOLD CAL THAT VALKO was at the pistol range. Apparently he'd decided that a rest wasn't needed. Cal had never talked to Valko's men because their leader was always present. He could see they were relaxed, something they hadn't exhibited around Valko. Maybe that was something.

Cal found Valko in the far left stall of the outdoor pistol range. By the number of casings on the ground, Cal estimated the Bulgarian was well into his fourth box of fifty rounds.

He waited until Valko finished shooting, extracted his magazine, inspected the open chamber, and set the pistol down on the wooden shelf. He didn't look up when he addressed Cal, but started reloading his magazines.

"What do you want?" asked Valko.

"What's your problem, Valko?"

The Bulgarian whirled around, eyes aflame. "What?"

"I said, what's your *fucking* problem?"

Valko took a step closer. Cal didn't flinch. They stood there for a few moments, the tension palpable. To Cal's surprise, Valko turned back to the range and continued loading his magazines. The Marine was sure they were about to come to blows. Part of him wanted to. Some bullies just need a good ass-kicking before they came around.

"We need to talk about this."

Valko ignored him.

Cal shook his head. He hated to do it, but maybe he should just call McMillan and tell him that the Bulgarians were out. Whatever.

He headed back toward The Lodge without another word. He was halfway there when a thought came.

Two minutes later he was knocking on the door of the room the Bulgarians were sharing. One of Valko's men, a dour-faced guy by the name of Georgi Levski answered.

"Do you mind if I come in?" asked Cal.

Levski nodded. The last Bulgarian, a skinny kid named Nikola Popov was sprawled out on a queen bed, reading an American porno mag. He glanced up when Cal entered but went right back to his perusal.

"Do you guys have a minute to talk?" asked Cal.

Levski shrugged and Popov put his magazine down, sliding to the edge of the bed to listen.

"Look, I know you guys are loyal to Valko, but we need to get some things figured out before we leave. Would you tell me what the hell the deal is with Valko?"

The Bulgarians looked at each other, Popov shaking his head as if to say, "We shouldn't say anything." Levski ignored him and answered Cal.

"There is something you must know about Stojan."

BARTELLA, IRAQ (APPROXIMATELY 22-MILES OUTSIDE MOSUL)

B usiness was good for Ali Kassab. The middle-aged vendor had more coin in his pocket than he'd had since the invasion in 2003. While many Iraqis cowered under the gaze of the advancing ISIS forces, his meat wagons supplied the army day and night. Ever since entering the country, Ali had nurtured the ISIS relationship, sometimes giving the jihadists whole shipments for free, knowing they would be grateful. And they were. Ali was one of the most popular visitors in the ever moving camps, one of the few outsiders who knew their locations.

While many thought the invading force engaged in indiscriminate killing, Ali knew better. He'd seen ISIS leaders killed by their chain of command for engaging in unsanctioned attacks. The West was trying to paint them as thugs, and many of them were, but fundamentally, they'd grown into something much more dangerous. Calculating. Trained. More sophisticated by the day.

It was better to make friends with such men, or at least

offer them something of value. What did an army need as much if not more than weapons and ammunition? Food and water.

ISIS lived off the land, obtaining supplies as they went. Unlike a conventional army, they had no supply train. But they were not pillaging. Their leaders knew that if they were to build the caliphate, they must have a land to rule. They were careful with what they took and only destroyed infrastructure in rare cases, usually to instill fear in a noncompliant populace.

The bells of his goats tinkled as he approached the well-lit guard post, crudely erected with large trucks serving as barriers. A high-powered light clicked on and shone right in his face. He'd been expecting it, and covered his eyes.

"Who is that?" asked a guard, his weapon undoubtedly pointed directly at the blinded supplier.

"It's Ali, you fool. Put that light down," said one of the guards.

The light was extinguished and Ali led his mule-drawn cart to the entrance.

"Good evening, Ammar. How is your duty this night?" asked Ali. One of the things that had amazed the Islamists was Ali's ability to remember names. He never had to be told twice, even remembering family members mentioned in passing.

"You come at a good time. We have more men coming every day. What did you bring us?" The guard moved around Ali to get a better look, knowing he would have first pick of the choicest supply. It was one of the few perks of standing watch.

"The usual. Lamb, beef, chicken and a barrel of fresh fish."

"Anything else?" asked the guard. Ali could imagine the man's mouth salivating.

"My cooler is filled with cheeses. Wheels and blocks. The

kind I have not found in many months. Would you like a sample?"

The guard nodded and Ali moved to the large cooler, surplus he'd purchased from an American supply sergeant four years before. It took up most of the cart, but kept his wares cold even under the relentless desert sun. He opened one of the side hatches and found the best of the bunch. Ali cut off two oversized hunks, each the size of a man's fist and handed one to each of the guards. They both bit into them hungrily. Ali smiled.

"And I have something else. Chocolate stolen from a Dutch freighter." He pulled out two aluminum-wrapped bars and handed them out. The men's eyes went wide. Too consumed with their meal, they waved Ali through, pointing to where the supply tent was.

He knew the way. Even though he hadn't been at this particular location, they always arranged things the same way. It wasn't five minutes before he'd found the kitchen tent nestled next to a much larger tent. Along the way he passed out treats from his seemingly never-ending supply, the men grateful when he thanked the ones he'd met by name. The new names he stored away.

"Ali! I was wondering if you would get here in time," said the fat supply chief who also doubled as one of the cooks. He was standing just outside the flap of the kitchen tent, hands on his hips, wearing a blood stained white apron.

"My apologies. It was slow going today. My mules were not happy with their cargo. Too much to pull."

The supply chief smiled. "Quickly. Tell me what you have. We have more guests coming tonight."

Ali's ears perked up at the comment. The whispers had been true.

Ali gave the man a rundown of what he'd brought, saving

the cheeses for last. He knew the overweight Syrian had a special love for good baladi.

Although his eyes betrayed his desire, the man knew how to negotiate. "I don't know if I have the money to pay for the extra items, Ali. Perhaps you could make me a deal?"

Ali smiled, having already prepared for the conversation. "Since you have been such a loyal customer, and friend, I wanted to give you the cheeses as a gift. A small thanks."

The man's eyes went wide. "That is very generous, I—"

Ali waved off the coming reply. "It is nothing. I got a good deal on the best meats, and I can only hope that when the glorious caliphate is born, I will continue to be one of your loyal servants."

The fat man walked over and hugged Ali. "Of course, my friend. Come. Let me get someone to unload your goods and I will get your payment."

Less than an hour later, Ali waved goodbye to the guards. They waved back enthusiastically, now accompanied by four others. The camp was expecting company. Ali whistled a tune as he walked beside his most stubborn mule, coaxing it with a soft lullaby. It was all he could do to not look back.

* * *

THE SUPPLY CHIEF STUFFED ANOTHER PIECE OF SOFT WHITE baladi cheese in his mouth. It had been too long since he'd savored such a delicacy. Because the army was constantly on the move, rationing was essential. Meals were simple and rarely fresh. That meant that even the man who controlled the food had to cut back. He was sure he'd lost at least ten pounds since leaving Syria. The thought made him rub his ample belly as he swallowed the cheese. It reminded him of his wife.

His master would be happy. He would save the cheese for

last and tell them that it hadn't cost a thing. His gift to the caliph.

He was distracted from his thoughts of home when one of his men dropped a serving platter. It sent the fat man into a tirade of curses. They had less than two hours before the caliph and his commanders arrived. Everything would have to be ready or it was his head. The caliph did not like his food to be served late.

To the fat man's delight, every course was met with a chorus of happy grunts and murmurs. Even the caliph had inquired about the source of the meal. Someone had pointed at the supply chief, who stood in the corner of the tent, stoically overseeing the service. He returned the caliph's nod proudly.

Finally, it came time for his surprise. He couldn't wait to see the look on the caliph's face. Maybe he would be invited to work at the palace once the new Islamic state was formed. One could hope.

He'd told his underlings not to touch the delicacies, wanting to parcel out the food with his own hand. The first one he grabbed was a large block of feta, probably two feet by two feet in size. He would serve it with the dates and figs he'd gotten from another vendor, and a collection of barreled olives he'd commandeered from a small town the day before.

The block was too big for a normal knife and he opted for a three foot carving knife they used to slaughter meat. It looked more like a sword than something you'd find in a kitchen.

He eased the blade into the center of the cheese, using two hands to shimmy it in. The blade stopped two inches down. The fat man's brow furrowed. He removed the blade and stuck his finger into the crevice he'd made. There was something hard in the middle of the cheese. He could feel it. *That Ali better not have given me rotting cheese.*

It was the last thought the fat man would ever have.

* * *

THE MASTER WAS IN THE SECOND VEHICLE OF THE FOUR truck convoy. They were late. There had been trouble with a group of prisoners who'd somehow escaped from a holding cell. His men had spent the afternoon running them down with their trucks, he among them.

He was tired and didn't feel like another meeting with the council. They always lasted late into the night and nothing ever seemed to get accomplished. The others wanted to be heard while the caliph sat listening, always patient.

Then, once the others departed, the caliph would speak to him alone. His verbal orders for The Master only. It was for the caliph that he came, not the others who always complained about his own increasing role in the regime.

He could see the lights of the temporary camp up ahead. The Master shook his head at the stupidity. It was a perfect target for aircraft if the Americans and their friends ever found the courage to act. Luckily, they hadn't, and the army of ISIS still moved with relative impunity.

They were two hundred yards from the entrance, their vehicles slowing, when The Master felt the rumble, followed by a massive explosion inside the camp, a plume rising from its midst. The truck skidded to a stop, the shockwave hitting them a split second later. It wasn't enough to do them any harm, but he could tell it was enough to destroy half of the camp.

"Tell the other vehicles to go and see what happened. We're going back," said The Master.

"But, Master, the caliph?" asked one of his deputies.

"If I am right, the caliph is dead. Now move."

His deputy nodded and got on the radio as the driver turned around and headed back toward Mosul. The Master knew what his men would find. If he was right, he was the new caliph.

* * *

THE MAN WHO WOULD SOON NO LONGER BE ALI KASSAB watched the inferno. There was no doubt that the ISIS leadership had been consumed. He said a silent prayer and pulled out the satellite phone he kept hidden under the cracked slats of his cart. There was only one phone number. He'd memorized it after reading it off the scribbled scrap of paper he'd found under his pillow days before.

He dialed the number, waiting anxiously for the man to pick up.

"Yes?"

"It is done."

"Are you sure?"

"Yes."

"Good. I will see you soon."

The call ended and Ibrahim Roubini threw the phone into the small fire he'd made in the crumbling stone hut. He waited until he was sure the phone was destroyed, and then went to prepare his cart. Now that the first salvo was fired, it was time to go home.

CAMP CAVALIER

Cal didn't know whether to punch a wall or beat Valko to a pulp. Of all the things he should've known... He'd almost picked up the phone and given Gen. McMillan an earful, but something in Cal still drew the line at being disrespectful to a Marine general.

He'd returned to the pistol range after talking to Valko's guys only to find the pile of spent rounds the Bulgarian had left. Asshole hadn't even had the courtesy to clean them up. It only added to Cal's anger.

He could've had someone find the guy, but Cal knew he needed time to think, to digest what he'd heard. The others would be looking to him, to see how he'd handle the situation. He had to be careful, deal with the Bulgarian one-on-one.

His mind swerved back to rage. How the hell could McMillan let a guy onto their team with a background like Valko's?

Cal stomped into The Lodge, not really paying attention

to where he was going. He needed a drink but couldn't have one. It would set a bad example. Besides, they had more to do, including the infiltration later that night.

The other teams, especially the drinkers, had taken to spending their off time in the bar. Without looking, Cal figured correctly that everyone except for the Bulgarians were in the large room. There were plenty of comfortable leather chairs, well worn and big enough for the largest operators. Some of them were napping as he entered. He nodded to Fox and Kreyling, who were hunched over a table with a stack of bar glasses, maneuvering them like soldiers on a battlefield.

Stefano Moretti was sitting at the bar, chatting with Gaucho. The Hispanic was trying to pick up a few words of Italian, and was laughing at the way Moretti was teaching him. Gaucho looked up as Cal entered and held his greeting when he saw Cal's face.

Cal found a chair in the corner, away from the others. Daniel watched him from across the room, always there. Cal ignored him.

As soon as Cal took a seat by himself, who else but Stojan "The Bloody Bulgarian" Valko walked into the lounge. Cal leaped out of his chair and approached Valko.

"You!" barked Cal, pointing his finger like a dagger at the Bulgarian.

Valko looked up, annoyance stamped on his features, but not really alarmed. "What?"

"You and me are gonna have a little talk...outside."

By that time Cal was standing right in front of his target, not a foot between them. Valko went to step back but Cal caught him by the front of the shirt. On instinct Valko's hand came down to grab Cal's wrist, but the Marine was already moving, his left hand coming around to deliver a vicious hook.

It never connected. Something had stopped his arm. Cal

pressed but his arm stayed where it was. He glanced to the left and saw MSgt Trent with his own massive arm wrapped around Cal's bicep.

"Let him go, Cal," said Trent.

Everyone else was on their feet.

"Stay out of this, Top," growled Cal.

"Cal, I think—"

Before Trent could finish, Valko's free arm whipped around, his fist aimed at Cal's exposed head. Cal braced for impact, but once again, the blow never landed.

It was Georgi Levski, one of Valko's guys who'd blocked the punch. Valko seethed, spittle running out of his mouth.

Levski said something to Valko in their native tongue. Valko's eyes bulged and his face rushed red. There was a brief exchange that no one understood. Cal was still holding Valko's shirt, Trent still holding Cal's arm, and everyone else watching.

It was Nikola Popov, the skinny Bulgarian, who said something and put a comforting hand on Valko's arm. That finally made Valko put his hands up, the Bulgarian looking almost contrite. Cal let go and backed away slowly, still ready.

"You wanna tell us what the hell is going on?" asked Trent, moving so that his massive frame stood between the two combatants. The others had moved closer, ready should the fight continue.

Cal glared at Valko. "You're out. As of this second you're gone."

Valko returned Cal's stare, looking like he might charge. His two men each had a hand on him, just in case. "What you think you know, eh?"

"You want me to say it here, in front of everybody?"

For some reason Valko's body relaxed. All of a sudden he looked deflated, like he was giving up. His gaze dropped to the ground. "Say it. They find out soon."

Cal paused for a moment, waiting. But he wasn't going to give Valko a pass. "Tell them about your brother, Valko. Your twin brother who's now a terrorist. Oh, and tell them about how he's part of a little gang we all know as ISIS."

There were murmurs from the others. They felt the same way Cal had when he'd been told. Furious. The tide had turned. Every face in the room looked to Valko, demanding an explanation.

"He is right. My brother left Bulgaria years ago and is now part of ISIS," said Valko, his eyes still averted.

"Do you mind telling us why the hell you didn't think this was worth mentioning?" asked Cal, ready to be done with the bastard.

Valko nodded. "It is complicated."

"You were recruited to help us wipe these guys off the face of the Earth. And now you're telling me that your brother is one of them? How are we supposed to trust you?"

Valko's head snapped up, his eyes burning, the intensity returned. "My brother has brought much dishonor to me and to my country. It is my duty to fix problem. Would you not do the same?"

"I don't know, Valko. Seems like you've been a world class prick ever since you got here, and that was before we knew your brother was a terrorist. Give me one good reason why I shouldn't have you shipped back to Bulgaria, or worse, locked up for questioning until this operation is over?" Cal had already made up his mind. Valko had to go. Too much of a liability and a liar on top of it. By the looks around the room, no one seemed to be taking Valko's side, even his own men.

"I give you good reason, Stokes." Valko paused and looked around the room, taking the time to make eye contact with each man. Then he said, "They call my brother *The Master*, and he is now caliph of ISIS."

CAMP CAVALIER

I t was like the air in the room was gone, everyone holding their breath. Shock, plain and simple. Not only was Valko's twin brother a terrorist, he was also the leader of ISIS? How was that even possible?

Once he could get his mouth to move, Cal asked, "I thought the caliph was Abdu—"

Valko shook his head. "My government send message just now. There is new video with my brother."

"Wait. You just said *new* video. You mean this isn't his first?"

"No. You see video with buckets of blood?"

"*That's* your brother?"

Valko nodded, his face still stern, but looking more like a boot lieutenant reporting in to a new unit. Nervous. Reading the vibe of the others.

Everyone in the room had seen the video of the lunatic pouring buckets of blood over himself and the soon-to-be chopped up priest. The damn video turned into a YouTube sensation before someone had had the balls to shut it down.

For the first time in a while, Cal didn't know what to say. Daniel spoke up for him.

"Why don't we take a look at the new video and see what Valko's talking about."

Cal was still speechless. How had this happened? He knew what he had to do. "Top, take Valko up to my room. Kreyling, I'd like for you and your men to accompany them."

The Brit nodded, his eyes boring holes into Valko.

"I'll be up there in a minute. I have a phone call to make," Cal said, motioning to Daniel, who followed him out.

CAL GOT LUCKY. EVEN THOUGH TRAVIS WAS OUT, GEN. McMillan was in a meeting with the president when he called. Two birds with one stone. There was shocked silence when Cal dropped the bomb about the Bulgarian's brother.

"Cal, first let me say I'm sorry. If we'd known—"

"I get it, General. Don't worry about it. I've had a couple minutes to think about it, and I think on some level I understand. Valko's brother somehow turned into the spawn of Satan and the guy wants to do the deed himself. Hell, if I was in his shoes I'd pull every damn string I could to get the assignment," said Cal.

"But that doesn't excuse the Bulgarians for dumping this in our lap," said the president. "I'm tempted to give their president a call."

"I'd say we hold off on that, Mr. President," suggest McMillan. "We're making some strides with their new leadership and I sure would like to have them on our side if this thing with Russia doesn't cool off."

"Okay. So what do you suggest?" asked Zimmer, obviously not pleased.

"Let me handle it," said Cal. "Maybe this is a blessing in disguise. I mean, who the hell could get us the goods on this guy better than his twin brother?"

"What do you think, General?"

"I think Cal's right. What we have on the guy is slim. We don't even have a real name for him other than *The Master*. The more information we can get the better."

"Against my better judgment, I'll go with your recommendation. I'm heading out within the hour, so if you need anything, Cal, please call General McMillan."

"No problem."

"And, Cal?"

"Yeah?"

"Don't do anything stupid," said Zimmer.

Cal laughed. "I'll try."

The call ended and Cal looked over at Daniel.

"What do you think?"

Daniel nodded. "You made the right call. Let's go see what Valko has to say. We can always lock him up if we have to."

IT WASN'T JUST MSGT TRENT AND THE BRITS GUARDING the Bulgarian in his spacious suite when he arrived. Every other man assigned to the mission was in the main room, facing the large flat screen TV mounted to the wall. Neil was fiddling with a set of wires and a laptop.

Gaucho joined Cal and Daniel when they walked in.

"Any news, boss?"

"Yeah. I'll tell everyone in a minute. I see you kept the others from coming?" asked Cal, somewhat annoyed at having a crowd in his room.

Gaucho shrugged. "Can you blame them?"

"No." Cal knew he would've done the same thing. Their mission hinged on the information they would hopefully gather from the Bulgarian. They were curious, but also as resentful as Cal about Valko's blatant omission. The warriors wanted to see what decision Cal would make, like Roman citizens waiting to see the thumbs-up or -down from the emperor. "What's Neil doing?"

"He found the video. We waited until you got here to play it," said Gaucho.

The television flickered to life and a still shot of the black and white ISIS flag popped up on the screen.

"Play it," said Cal, moving to stand behind where Valko sat sandwiched between Trent and Kreyling on the couch.

The video began and the face of The Master, Valko's twin brother, appeared. Now that Cal looked closer, he could see the resemblance. The similarities were there if you knew that the man in robes and thick beard was related to the gruff Bulgarian sitting in front of the television.

The Master began in his adopted tongue, the translation in yellow letters across the screen. "Today some of our greatest warriors have returned to Allah's side. In an act of treachery, they were murdered by the infidels of the west, sending them early to bask in Allah's grace. We pray for their loss, but we stand stronger than before. Our blessed army grows larger by the day. Beware to the infidel who steps in our path."

The Master paused, his face becoming more solemn. "I have been chosen to lead our cause, in Allah's name. As the new caliph of the Islamic state, I promise to bring Allah's will to the world. To the murderers who killed our brothers, I say this — you are no longer safe. We will find you and kill you. To those who think to oppose us, do not. For those who wish to join us, you have only to ask. The caliphate of Islam is made of brothers from around the world. Iraqis, Syrians, Egyptians, we come to Allah's call. Jordanians, Saudis and

Indians coming together. Even our brothers from the West heed Allah's call."

The camera zoomed in closer, The Master's eyes now burning with intensity. "So you see, we are everywhere. Allah's warriors, waiting and watching. To the infidels, I give one final warning. This battle does not have borders. We come closer each day to striking the heart of your impure world. To my brothers living under the hateful eye of the infidel, I say rise up! You do not need to be with us to be *with us*. Find others and throw off your chains of bondage. Because if it is Allah's will, it is Allah's will."

The video went back to the image of the ISIS flag.

"So that's your brother?" asked Cal.

"Yes," said Valko, his mood unreadable.

"How about you tell us his story. I'd love to know how the brother of an elite Bulgarian operator ended up being the most wanted man on Earth."

There were nods around the room. Everyone wanted to know.

"Can I have drink first?" asked Valko.

Cal couldn't see anything wrong with a little liquid courage. Hell, their night op was probably shot anyway. Who was going to be able to keep their minds on task if the Bulgarian problem was still out there? Cal walked over to his well-stocked bar and poured three fingers of scotch in a rocks glass. He gave it to Valko, who downed it in one gulp, handing the glass back to Cal.

Valko nodded his thanks and began his tale.

* * *

THE MASTER WAS BORN KIRIL VALKO MINUTES BEFORE HIS identical twin brother, Stojan. Raised in a strict military family, Kiril and Stojan were inseparable from birth. Their childhood was full of adventure as they moved from one military installation to the next. By the time their father made sergeant in the Bulgarian army, Kiril and Stojan were five years old.

Their mother worked in officers's houses to make ends meet and the two brothers were often left alone. They played war, Kiril insisting on being the shining knight while Stojan took up the mantle of the barbarian horde.

By the time they were ten, the boys saw less and less of their father. Stojan found out later that the elder Valko had been selected for the 68th Special Forces Brigade, something he wasn't supposed to know. The unit kept him away for months at a time, always unscheduled.

While Stojan tried to emulate everything his father said or did, his brother went for books and immersed himself in schooling. They still played together, but things started to change. They were twins, but they had differing outlooks on what their worlds would become. Stojan wanted to be a soldier while Kiril yearned to be a scholar or maybe even a professor.

The day after the boys turned thirteen there was a phone call for their mother. She was out buying food, so Stojan answered. The man on the other line said it was important to speak to Mrs. Valko right away, that her husband had been hurt.

It turned out that Senior Sergeant Valko (equivalent of a U.S. Army Sergeant First Class) had shattered both legs in an alpine skiing accident. They went to see him in the hospital, but he'd yelled at their mother until she'd ushered the twins away in tears.

It only got worse from there. Even though their father was being hailed as a hero, having saved the lives of eight of his men before falling into the ravine, his mood darkened. Unable to return to his unit, he was given a desk job. A quarter bottle of liquor a night increased to a half, then a whole. It was rare that he was sober.

At first he just stumbled around the house on his stiff legs, cursing at unseen shadows. Then the beatings began. Every day he would come home from work, already half drunk, demanding a meal. Their mother would comply without a word, while her husband drank himself into a rage. Plates were smashed, and then his belt came off as he whipped away at his wife.

The first time it happened, Stojan stood transfixed. The second time Kiril ran to his mother's aid. No match for his father's strength, it was Kiril who felt the first real blows. Stojan sat on the floor crying as his brother looked at him from a fetal position, the kicks and punches raining down. He never said a word, always keeping his eye on his brother, willing him to stay out of it.

The next day Stojan walked to school alone, his mother nursing her bloodied and bruised eldest. Stojan chastised himself for not stepping in, not helping his brother. But he was torn. He wanted to be just like his father, a hero. But what he'd done...

That afternoon, Stojan ran home to see his brother. Kiril wasn't there. His mother said he'd gone to church. Stojan sprinted the mile to the small chapel where the Valkos occasionally went to mass. Kiril was sitting in the front row, head bowed, lips moving in a silent prayer.

Stojan didn't want to disturb his brother, and took a seat next to him, waiting. Finally, Kiril looked up, the deep purple bruises on his face dark in the limited candlelight. It made Stojan want to cry.

"I have talked to God," said Kiril. "He says you will be safe."

Stojan hadn't known what to say and simply nodded, not understanding what his brother meant. Not another word was said, and they left the church together, Stojan helping his brother, whose body still ached from the beating.

After that day Stojan saw less and less of his brother. Kiril buried himself in schoolwork, often staying well into the night to study. He was well-liked and had no shortage of friends. Stojan was the opposite, Kiril being his only playmate.

When Kiril was home, their father would repeat his attacks, never targeting Stojan. Always his mother first, then Kiril. It was as if his father was baiting Kiril to act, and act he did.

The abuse lasted well into their sixteenth year. By then Stojan's father had been medically retired from the Army and was living off his pension. He got fatter and fatter, and drunker and drunker. Mad at the world for where he'd ended up, the elder Valko raked his wrath over his oldest son.

One day Stojan returned home from rugby practice to find the house empty. It was well past dinner time and no one was there, no meal waiting. He thought it was strange but was too hungry to think about it. As he scrounged for something to eat, he heard a siren's wail through the open window. It got closer and soon he saw the flashing lights of a military police vehicle in their dirt driveway. Living outside the Novo Selo Range, a joint Bulgarian/NATO base, military vehicles weren't uncommon.

Stojan went to the front door and met the two military policemen on the front stoop.

"Stojan Valko?" one of the men asked.

"Yes."

"Come with us please."

"But I—"

"You're not in trouble. It's your brother."

His brother? Stojan couldn't think of any time the perfect

Kiril had ever gotten in trouble. *He* was the one always skipping class and getting in fights, not Kiril.

Worried, he got in the back of the vehicle and they sped off toward the army base, siren blaring.

When they got to the station, Stojan was taken to his mother. She looked like she'd seen a ghost, and it took a moment before she noticed him standing in front of her. When she did, she looked at him, touched his face, and then walked away.

Stojan looked up at the army major who'd escorted him in. "I don't understand. What happened?"

The major shook his head. "Your brother was arrested, and—"

"I know that! I asked what happened!"

The major didn't lose his temper, a gesture that made Stojan even more frightened.

The officer said, "Your father was visiting some old comrades on base. Your brother followed him and shot him. Your father is dead, Stojan."

Stojan couldn't believe what he was hearing. Kiril had never lifted a hand in anger, even against his father. After much pleading, the major reluctantly took him back to where they were holding his brother, in an interrogation room handcuffed to a thick wooden table covered in graffiti.

He walked in, unable to speak, taking in the look on his brother's face. He looked at peace.

Kiril didn't say a word as Stojan fumbled with the chair across from his brother. The major left them alone. The seconds ticked by.

They sat there for what seemed like hours, neither one talking. Finally, Stojan looked across at his brother and asked, "Why?"

Kiril smiled and said, "I told you. I had to keep you safe."

AFTER THE AUTHORITIES FOUND OUT ABOUT THE YEARS OF abuse, things settled down. While the military could press charges, the incident was downgraded from cold blooded murder to self-defense. After all, what soldier wouldn't feel for the victim of such circumstances? The military did not want a scandal.

Kiril was given a relative slap on the wrist, sentenced to a year in civilian prison. He asked to be put in solitary confinement, and his request was granted. Kiril would have occasional contact with other inmates, but for the most part he would be alone. He forbade his brother to visit, something that wounded Stojan deeply.

A year later Kiril emerged a changed man. Sporting a scraggly beard, Stojan almost didn't recognize his twin brother. Kiril said he'd found his answers, that his time in prison had been well-spent. In a rare moment of openness, Kiril explained that he'd befriended a group of men in jail who had showed him the path of Allah. As if he realized what he'd just said, Kiril didn't say another word about his confinement.

Instead of finishing high school, he applied for a scholarship to study in Lebanon. They'd said their farewells at the airport, and Kiril boarded the plane with a small group of similarly dressed students. Stojan wouldn't see his brother for another five years.

Meanwhile, Stojan barely finished high school, and then he enlisted in the army. Finally finding his home, he rose through the ranks quickly, besting his peers and garnering the notice of senior officers.

It wasn't until he was applying for a position with his father's old unit, the 68th Special Forces Brigade, that Stojan heard his brother's name.

He was called into the adjutant's office one day and questioned at length about his family. Sergeant Valko told the officer everything he knew, including when he'd last seen his brother. The captain had looked at him with disdain.

"Are you aware that your brother, Kiril, is now affiliated with Hezbollah in Lebanon and has suspected ties with other terrorist organizations in the Middle East?"

Valko was speechless. "I...I don't understand. My brother is a scholar. He went to Lebanon on an academic scholarship."

The captain laughed at him, an act that almost sent Valko flying over the desk to throttle the man.

"Tell me, Sergeant Valko, did you or did you not know that your brother is at this very moment visiting associates here in Bulgaria?"

"Of course not. I—"

"So he has not made any attempt to see you, and you have made no attempt to see him?"

"No, sir."

The captain stared at him for an extended moment, and then nodded.

"Very well. If he should try to contact you, call me at this number. Remember where your loyalties lie."

The officer tore off a piece of paper and handed it to Valko.

"You are dismissed."

LATER THAT NIGHT HE'D VISITED A BAR OFF BASE TO TRY TO clear his head. He couldn't believe what the captain had told him. There was no way his brother was the enemy. The Kiril he knew was kind and thoughtful, a man he sometimes wished to be himself.

Just as he'd ordered another drink, someone tapped him on the shoulder. He turned and moved back in shock. The man standing before him was clean-cut and well-dressed in a suit and tie. He almost didn't recognize Kiril, who now looked down at him with the same smirk he'd had as a child.

"What are you doing here?" Stojan hissed.

Kiril's smile slipped for a moment, but returned just as fast. "Am I not allowed to see my twin brother?" He went to embrace Stojan, but the soldier pushed him away.

"Get away from me."

The smile disappeared. "I see that you've turned out just like our father," said Kiril, his eyes burning in a way Stojan had never seen.

"And I see that you've turned into one of those jihadists!"

Kiril moved closer and whispered, "Who told you that?"

Stojan glared at his brother. "Does it matter? I can see by the look on your face that it is true."

People were starting to stare and Kiril noticed, motioning for his brother to quiet down.

"You don't know what you're talking about, brother. There is a war being waged that will soon—"

"I don't want to hear about your Allah. Get out of here before I call the police."

Kiril moved as if to say something, but nodded instead. He cast one more look at his brother, and left.

It was the last time Stojan Valko would ever talk to his brother.

CAMP CAVALIER

No tears. Stojan Valko just sat there when he'd finished his tale, the soft spin of the fan overhead the only sound in the room.

Everyone waited, digesting what they'd just heard. Cal couldn't imagine what was going through Valko's head. He understood why the Bulgarian had ended up the way he was. You didn't become one of the best by feeling sorry for yourself. There were two ways to go, wallow or fight. Valko was a fighter. Begrudgingly, Cal had to respect that.

But it didn't change the fact that the man had lied. It put Cal in an uncomfortable position. These men were looking to him for the answer, to make the hard call. A year earlier he probably would have removed Valko from the team without digging deeper. Things had changed. He had changed.

Cal wasn't ready to make a decision. There were questions to be asked.

"Tell me how you got a spot on this team. You said your government knows about your brother," said Cal.

Valko nodded. "My brother's choice has come up many times. I have had to work hard to prove that I am not my brother. This time, I ask my president for favor. I saved his life, so he lets me come, and says he will not tell your president about Kiril."

To everyone's surprise, it was the Japanese, Takumi Kokubu, who spoke up. "How do we know we can trust you?"

Cal had learned that of all the countries in the world, Japan possibly maintained the strictest control over the influx of Muslims and Arabs. Xenophobic to a certain degree, their approach to extremism was to stop it at the source. If you didn't have a certain race or religion in your country, the chance of a surprise attack was considerably lessened. The Japanese were cautious. They'd learned their lesson after the Second World War, and didn't plan on losing again.

Valko met the Japanese leader's eyes. "I know what you think, that I am bad person. But think of what I do. My twin is my shadow. Always haunting. Less promotion because of him. Less trust because of him. Less honor because of him. I work hard. Be the best. My men know this. My government know this. But still the shadow. You want Valko to beg? No. Only one thing I can do."

"And what is that?" asked Kokubu.

"Kill my brother."

The comment hung in the air like a spinning blade, Valko's intent clear. And yet, Cal saw the doubt in the men's eyes. He didn't blame them. But something told the Marine that maybe this is what they needed. A pit bull is deadly because it never lets go, not until it takes its last breath. That was Valko. He'd dedicated his life to finding and killing his twin. And he wouldn't stop until he had.

While others might find it vile and inhumane, Cal understood, and he figured the others would in time. The problem was Valko's attitude. Even though he'd spilled his guts, the man didn't show more than a glimmer of remorse. He wasn't sorry, truly. He'd done what he felt he had to do. Again, something Cal could respect. It pissed him off that Valko did it on Cal's watch, but that was a moot point now.

Cal made up his mind. "Here's the deal. Valko stays." There were murmurs from the group, the Brits and Italians the most vocal. He even saw Kokubu scowl. Cal put a hand in the air to cut off the chatter. "Look, I'm as ticked off about what Valko did as you are, but we're here for a reason. We need to stop ISIS. Whatever you think of Valko, can any one of you tell me that he, maybe more than the rest of us, has the most to lose if we fail?"

There were glares, but no one said a word.

Cal continued. "Here's my only request. Valko, I can be a hard-headed prick from time to time, but, dude, you take that act to a whole other level. If you're gonna stick around here, you need to fix the attitude and be part of the team."

More murmurs, but this time of agreement.

Valko nodded, and then to Cal's surprise, replied with a thin smile. "I can do this."

"Good. Now let's get our stuff together. The helos are coming to get us at sundown."

Cal waited for everyone to file out of the room. He got dirty looks from Kreyling, and more of an exasperated roll of the eyes from Moretti as they left. Kokubu stayed.

Once everyone was gone, it was just Cal, Daniel and the Japanese in the room. Kokubu had his hands clasped behind his back like a pacing school teacher.

"Cal, I did not want to bring this up in front of the others, but I must strongly protest the Bulgarians being allowed to stay. Can you not see the security risk?" asked Kokubu.

Cal nodded. "I know. But there aren't a lot of us. If nothing else, Valko can give us more insight into his brother's tactics, maybe even his motives. I'm sure the Bulgarian government has a dossier on the guy. Maybe this is a blessing in disguise."

Kokubu thought about it for a moment. "That is possible, but you must promise me that you'll do everything in your power to keep him contained. I made an oath to my countrymen that I would see to their well-being. To me, having Valko with us goes against my word."

"I understand your concern, and I appreciate you telling me. Here's what I will promise you. I will use everything at my disposal to put pressure on the Bulgarian government to give us anything they have on Valko's brother. Trust me, my president is about as happy about this as you are, and he'll be more than pleased to make the phone call. Plus, I'll keep an eye on Valko. I made the call, so he's my problem now."

Cal couldn't tell whether he'd instilled confidence in Kokubu or not. The serious operator was a hard man to read.

"Very well," said Kokubu. "I've heard that you are an honorable man, Stokes-san. Do not let Stojan Valko tarnish your character." He nodded to Cal and Daniel, and left the room.

Cal looked at Daniel after the door closed. "Well, here we go again. Another clusterfuck and we haven't even stepped off yet."

Daniel chuckled. "Just like the Corps."

Cal smiled. "Just like the Corps."

MOSUL, IRAQ

3:20AM AST, AUGUST 14TH

The trucks rolled into the city as Mosul's citizens slept. There were thirty in all, empty cargo holds, drivers alert, their orders clear. Entering from the east side of town, the vehicles drove through roundabouts and intersections escorted by captured armored personnel carriers and HUMVEEs. No force moved to stop them. The caliph had seen to that.

The Ninevah Ruins passed on their left as the destination neared. Minutes later they slowed as they approached the entrance to the University of Mosul campus. Two guards waved them through, friends of the cause. Grim smiles and a nod were all that was shared. Over 30,000 students were said to be enrolled at the university, but it was not yet the fall semester. Those already in attendance would be asleep, but not for long.

Roads clear, they made their way to the dormitories, still no opposition. They pulled up next to the eight buildings that looked like a linear apartment complex. Armed men poured out of the personnel carriers, brandishing a mixture of Kalishnikovs and captured M-16s. None masked. Half of them secured the perimeter, while the others moved toward the dorms.

There were clicking sounds as a P.A. system came to life from the bed of the lead personnel carrier. Its siren sounded, prompting a smattering of lights to come on from inside the dormitories. Faces peeked out cautiously.

"In the name of Allah and by order of his appointed caliph, you are to exit your rooms and move to our trucks."

The command was repeated three more times, a stream of bleary eyed students making their way out onto the sidewalk and down to the street. They were confused. When they'd looked out their windows, most of the students had assumed that the formation was made up of the Iraqi troops who'd been sent to secure the school. They were sorely mistaken.

The trouble had begun months before, in the spring. Just when things seemed settled, ISIS exerted their power on the school. Two weeks earlier, the professors and deans of the university were summoned into a meeting with ISIS leaders and told that men and women were no longer allowed to mix, both in and out of classes. It was a blow for the second largest university in Iraq, which boasted over one hundred fields of study. All of a sudden they'd been forced to take a step back in time. Modern in many respects, the school had no option except to comply.

Women averted their eyes at the sight of the armed men, shuffling arm-in-arm with their friends. The male students looked shocked, as if they'd woken to a bad dream that would soon be over. It wouldn't.

The first load of students departed twenty minutes later, a score of ISIS warriors staying behind to guard the remaining students, who were told to sit on the ground.

The trucks made their way west, where less than ten

minutes later they came to the open gate of the marina belonging to the Al-Sadeer Tourist Complex on the banks of the Tigris. Students were ordered to get off the bus and follow the path toward the river, the path illuminated in the foggy morning by crooked lampposts, eerie sentinels under whose gaze they marched.

Armed militants guided them to a dock where the first five male students were ushered forward. At the end of the dock stood a man with a black mask holding a pistol. Another masked man stood behind him with a basket full of extra magazines.

The first student was pushed forward by his escort, stumbling as he neared the water's edge. The man with the gun helped him up with one hand, almost friend-like, then put the pistol to the student's head and fired, the body crumpling. As he fell, he was pushed into the flowing river by the escort who'd been expecting the shot. Their timing was perfect.

The gunman motioned for another and another. And so it went for the next hour. Round after round. Student after student. No one begged. Only silent tears were shed. They saw their fate and were only occasionally prodded forward by the escorts. Blood made the dock slick where the shots were made. Three times they had to call for a bucket and a mop. The gunman and escorts were caked in gore, but didn't seem to mind.

Six hundred bodies now floated south on the Tigris as the ISIS troops loaded back into their vehicles and made the return trip to the university. They would make another three trips that morning, the river soon clogged with the dead.

THE WHITE HOUSE

The president had already seen the video. He'd been asleep when the secret service agent knocked lightly on his bedroom door, delivering the laptop with the macabre reel waiting. There was no narration this time. The Master did not make an appearance.

It began with a simple message in red lettering over a white background.

For Allah and our dead brothers, let the slaughter of non-believers begin.

He didn't watch the whole thing. It was over two hours of film, at first dark from the early morning footage and gradually growing lighter as the morning wore on. One by one the innocent were slain and thrown unceremoniously into the Tigris. Like a farmer shucking corn, the ISIS militants went about their job like it was the most normal thing in the world.

They only paused to reload, and there was plenty of ammunition.

President Zimmer was now sitting in the Oval Office watching what news anchors were saying around the globe. The video spread quickly, but to Zimmer's dismay, there didn't seem to be much of an outcry. Thousands of innocent students had just been killed and Americans didn't care.

Temper rising, his foot tapped on the ground as he waited for his guests to arrive. Travis Haden was the first to show, followed shortly by Gen. McMillan. Five minutes later his national security advisor, press secretary and the director of the CIA stepped in, each taking their seats without a word.

"Have you all seen the video?" the president asked.

They all nodded.

"What do you think?"

The former news anchor turned press secretary, Bob Lundgren, spoke first.

"Same thing as before, Mr. President. Crazy jihadists murdering innocent people."

Zimmer's eyes narrowed. "You don't seem to be too disgusted with it, Bob."

Lundgren shrugged. "What do you want me to say, that it's awful? Sure, it's bad."

Zimmer normally liked the outgoing Lundgren, but today he wanted to punch him. The president pointed at Lundgren.

"That's what's wrong with this country. We see a video like that and we just take it."

"What do you want us to do? It's not like we can stop every lunatic on the planet," said Lundgren, not an ounce of his famous confidence lost. He was used to being top dog, and up until that very moment, he and the president had always been on the same side. It was clear to Zimmer that Lundgren hadn't figured out the president wanted answers, not commentary.

"Bob, I'm sorry I called you in. I'd like to talk to the others for a few minutes. I'll let you know what we decide."

"But—"

"Thanks, Bob." It was a dismissal, and finally Lundgren got it. He stood and left without saying another word.

"I'm sorry you had to see that, gentlemen. It was my mistake inviting him, but I thought that maybe he could help us come up with something to say to the public. I was wrong," said Zimmer.

No one said a word, instead waiting for him to continue.

"Doug, what are you getting from your people on the ground?"

Doug Sizer, the new CIA Director, took off his reading glasses and said, "Our sources say that thirty trucks plus security vehicles entered the University of Mosul campus at approximately 3:30am Mosul time. The witnesses they could find said that the loading was orderly and that a total of four trips were made. By the images we've collected from the video, we're pretty sure the killing was done at the Al-Sadeer Tourist Complex."

"Do we know why they targeted the university?" asked Zimmer.

"More bang for their buck, Mr. President. Instead of having to go knocking door-to-door, it was as simple as asking the students to file out of their dorms. They wanted to make a statement, and they did."

"And they just waltzed in there completely unopposed? What about the Iraqi police and the military?"

"We think university guards were recruited to let them through. When my people went to investigate, every guard-house was empty. No signs of struggle. As for the military...we still don't have an answer."

Zimmer shook his head. They'd spent billions equipping and training the Iraqis and now this. It was getting worse.

First they fled and now they were letting their own people, hell, their own children, die! Something had to be done, and soon.

"Trav, where are we with Cal's team?"

"They're finalizing things right now and prepping to leave tonight," said Travis.

"Did we get the dossier from the Bulgarians?"

The director of the CIA nodded. "Yes, sir. A courier brought it to my house earlier today. I haven't had a chance to hand if off to my analysts."

"Make sure you keep Travis and General McMillan in the loop. Trav, you get the pleasant duty of keeping your cousin informed."

Everyone nodded.

"Now, tell me what the hell we're going to do about the Iraqis."

Gen. McMillan answered, "We always knew this was a long-term play, Mr. President. Lundgren was right that we can't stop every lunatic in the world, but we do have an obligation to help our allies."

"What if our allies are so distracted by their own inner squabbles that they can't take care of themselves?" asked Zimmer, disgusted by the ongoing frustrations with Iraq and Afghanistan. When religion and race were thrown into the mix, and tribal loyalties added as the icing on the cake, Zimmer couldn't see any good coming out of the situation.

While he'd been cautiously optimistic about their chances before stepping into the Oval Office, now he was downright fatalistic. They couldn't get their act together, and ISIS, the Taliban and al-Qaeda were taking advantage. It had to stop.

Travis said, "We can't force our beliefs on them. We've had that discussion a hundred times. To assume that they'll spawn a working democracy overnight is insane."

"It's been over ten years," protested the president's

national security advisor, a short academic named Ivan Winger.

"How do you expect the Iraqis to change thousands of years of customs? It won't work. They are not us. We've given them training, gear and money. We helped rebuild their infrastructure. But have we really given them the incentive to do it themselves? I hate to talk bad about the last president, but he had withdrawal on the mind, not empowerment. It's like our welfare system. Where's the incentive to stop living on the government's dime? They're doing the same thing with us."

Winger sat up straighter, his face burning scarlet. "I think that's extraordinarily unfair. We worked hard to help the Iraqis. For you to say that the only thing we wanted to do was run—"

Travis interrupted the man's babbling and addressed the president. "Look, I've talked this over with General McMillan, and we think it's time to pull a Teddy Roosevelt."

Zimmer grinned, seeing the look of determination in Travis's eyes. That was the reason he kept the SEAL and McMillan close. They were men of action, and action was what was needed.

"Tell me more."

CAMP CAVALIER

Cal was the last to go through the chow line, heaping a healthy mound of old fashioned hash browns and a stack of pancakes on his partitioned tray. Who knew when they'd next get a decent meal?

When he turned to find a seat, he was glad to see how the rest of his international team had situated. For days they'd kept to themselves, Brits mingling with Brits and Japanese hanging with Japanese. That had changed.

It was funny what going operational does to interpersonal relationships. It either widens the divide or melds the bond. Cal was happy to see that the once wary teams were coming together. On the eve of battle, they'd need every shred of brotherhood they could find to kill the enemy and come back in one piece. Maybe it was something about the possibility of death or the bond forged through shared adversity.

Either way, Cal would never take credit. They'd all worked hard and come together as a team. Even the Bulgarians were coming around. Valko had kept his mouth shut on the insertion and had complimented Cal when they'd finished. It had shocked the hell out of Cal, but Daniel had merely nodded when they talked about it on the drive back from the training area.

As Cal approached, he chuckled when he heard Moretti peppering Kokubu with questions. Once again the Japanese had surprised them all, slipping into the enemy compound undetected and taking out the head "bad guy" before he knew what happened. MSgt Trent said they were like ninjas. Cal agreed. There was more to the Kokubu and his team than any of them knew. *Medics my ass.*

After their debriefing, Cal talked to the team of SSI operators who'd been kind enough to play the terrorist role, and he'd been pleased to learn that their movement had, for the most part, gone undetected. It was impossible to stay invisible forever, but that's what bullets and explosives were for. They'd used simulation rounds and effectively took out the entire veteran opposition force.

"Looks like you've got a good team there, Cal. Good luck," the head of SSI's training department had said. Coming from the crusty former Green Beret, that was a helluva compliment.

Cal sat down next to Daniel and took a look at his men. They looked tired, but happy. It was the look a warrior got when they knew they'd done well, exceeded expectations. Bottom line: they were ready.

AFTER BREAKFAST, THEY HEADED OUTSIDE. CAL LED THE way, hiking up a small rise that overlooked Camp Cavalier, SSI's second headquarters. There was a sign nailed to a tree at the top of the hill that said,

For Those Who Have Gone Before Us, May They Continue To Serve
As Our Guardian Angels.

Cal didn't know who'd left the hand painted sign, but it seemed fitting. He thought of his father, Marine Colonel Calvin Stokes, who'd led his Marines with bravery and a resolute heart. He thought of Brian Ramirez, the former Navy Corpsmen, who'd died in the mountains of Wyoming on an SSI operation to rescue Neil Patel. Lost Marines. Lost friends. Lost family.

Over time he'd come to realize they might not be standing at his side, but they'd always be with him. He could never forget the lessons he'd learned from his father, or the way Ramirez wouldn't hesitate to come to the aid of a friend. Some part of them would always be there.

So the crude sign was fitting as the rest of the men made their way up the hill, taking in the view of the surrounding countryside. They were his new friends and soon-to-be brothers in war and bloody battle.

"I wanted to bring you all up here to say thank you. I know we haven't all seen eye-to-eye on everything—"

"You've got that right!" said Gene Kreyling with a laugh.

Cal chuckled with the others. "Yeah. Funny how this whole thing started out. Nobody said putting a bunch of knuckle draggers together was easy. We come from different lands, different backgrounds, even different beliefs. But I think we can all agree that we all see the difference between good and evil, right and wrong. You came because you believe that it's worth risking your life to fight evil, to destroy it wherever it rears its ugly head. As we've seen throughout our careers, evil takes many shapes. Luckily for us, we know what our enemy looks like. We've seen the videos and know their intent. Some of us may not come back, but I will say that I'm proud to be with you, until the end if need be."

Cal paused, searching for the right words. He didn't want to be preachy or overly sentimental, but the words had come from the heart. He looked around at those gathered, grim faces, ready to take the fight to the enemy.

He opened his mouth to continue, but Stojan Valko spoke up first, a thin smirk punctuating his words.

"I think what you want to say, Cal, is let's kill those sons of bitches."

Cal grinned. *Yeah. Goddamned right.*

CHARLOTTESVILLE, VIRGINIA

Cal could barely hear what Diane was saying. His mind was elsewhere, his eyes on hers. He caught snippets of what she was talking about between bites of food. Her lips glowed, making him blink more than once. The way she smiled with her mouth and her eyes.

"Cal."

The sound of his name shook him from his thoughts.

"Sorry, what?" he asked.

She cocked her head to the side.

"Are you okay?" asked Diane, placing her fork on the table, wiping a bit of salad dressing from the corner of her perfect lips.

"Yeah. Sorry. Just a little distracted. A lot on my mind."

Cal stabbed his salad, trying unsuccessfully to snag a cherry tomato, finally giving up and setting his fork down, too.

"Is this about your trip?" she asked.

He'd told her that he was going out of town on business.

No details, just that he might be gone for a while. She'd merely nodded, didn't press.

"A little bit of that, and a lot of little or no sleep." That was the truth. There hadn't been time for a nap after the night exercise. He'd given the rest of the team the day to rest and get prepped. They were big boys and didn't need handholding. Most of their gear would be waiting for them overseas, so really it was just a matter of repacking the stuff they'd brought from their respective countries.

Cal had called Diane at the last minute and asked if she had time for an early dinner, explaining that he'd be leaving for D.C. in a matter of hours. Luckily she'd said yes. He didn't want to leave without saying goodbye.

He couldn't explain what he was feeling. If Dr. Higgins had asked him, Cal probably would've said he felt disjointed, in no way second-guessing his decision to hit ISIS, but... Well, he guessed that he was getting a small taste of what his father and other married troops felt before leaving their loved ones. It was an uncomfortable feeling, something he wasn't used to.

"What time do you leave?" asked Diane.

"I'm driving up to D.C. at seven, to miss the rush hour traffic."

Again, she didn't ask where he was going, and didn't ask why he was being aloof.

"Can I ask you something?"

"Sure."

"Look, I know you can't tell me what you're doing, and that's fine. I get it. I come from that world. But could you do me a favor?"

Cal nodded, worried she was going to make him promise something he couldn't deliver. *Right now I'd do almost anything for her. She just gets me.*

Diane reached out and took his hand, looking at him with those piercingly beautiful eyes, loving, kind, smart.

"Just let me know you're okay."

"I will."

* * *

CAL DIDN'T HAVE TIME TO WALK HER HOME, SO THEY SAID their goodbyes outside the restaurant. A hug and lingering kiss, the kind of goodbye you give someone when you don't know where your relationship stands, and yet, you have no idea when you'll see them again.

He watched her go. Twice she looked over her shoulder and smiled, soon disappearing in the throng of students heading to and from the corner for dinner.

A moment later, Daniel materialized next to him.

"Everything okay?" he asked.

"Yeah. I think so."

* * *

MOSUL, IRAQ - 1:03AM AST, AUGUST 15TH

At almost the same moment, Hasan al-Mawsil was saying his own goodbyes. The four priests each presented him with a gift, something to help him on his journey. Food. Water. A wooden cross on a leather strap. And a satellite phone.

Hasan didn't think he'd be coming back and that was okay. He wasn't sorry. Mosul had too many memories, too many ghosts that haunted him at every turn. Hasan thanked the kind priests and slipped out of the hideout, the darkness complete as he made his way to the rendezvous point.

Over the last two days, he'd met with the Jews on three more occasions. He didn't necessarily trust them, but understood the benefits of having a common enemy. They'd told him about the attack on the ISIS leadership, their smiles wide as they described the exploits of their countryman. Patient, those Jews, and ruthless.

"That is what we need, Hasan. We need to do what we can to help penetrate their army, hit them in unexpected ways. They must think that the opposition is everywhere," Timothy had said.

It sounded good at the time, but Hasan had witnessed the retribution ISIS's new caliph leveled against the Iraqi people. The mass murder at the University of Mosul was only the beginning. No longer were they targeting specific groups; labels didn't matter. The message was clear: *You are either with us or against us*.

Hasan had heard of at least three insider attacks, two in local police stations and one in a military outpost. In each case, a supposed ally had turned on his men, slaughtering as many as he could until he was killed himself.

The death toll was rising. Iraqis who'd once turned a blind eye to the atrocities, holding more of an 'it's not my problem' attitude, were now watching ISIS with mounting alarm. There had always been the problem of sectarian violence, Sunni against Shia. Radicals against moderates. Muslims against non-Muslims. The divides were many and had been for as long as humans inhabited the Mesopotamian region.

But the killing of the university students had changed everything. Not only had Christians been killed, so too had foreigners and followers of Islam. ISIS was no longer asking for volunteers, it was join them or die.

It made Hasan wonder how long it would take the fragmented Iraqi population to wake up, or if they ever would. The Kurds knew how to take care of themselves. He'd had enough interaction with the people in the north to know they would fight to the death before they allowed outside forces to take over their land. Hasan knew the Kurds stood the best chance of surviving, having already held off ISIS forces with the help of air support from the Americans and their allies.

It was the rest of Iraq that Hasan worried about. His people. Always fighting. To the eyes of the world, the coalition victory and march through Baghdad in 2003 marked a much-needed change in Iraqi leadership, a triumph to celebrate. While some things changed, the underlining tension did not.

As he made his way to the meet-up with the Israelis, Hasan prayed that his people would put aside their differences, stand as one, or die trying.

JOINT BASE ANDREWS

Everyone's gear had been stowed on the C-17 Globemaster III that would be taking them straight into Baghdad. They were scattered against the bulkhead, having plenty of room in the fifty-plus seats. Some of the men were already settling in, blankets and jackets balled up as pillows, headphones plugged in, time to sleep.

MSgt Trent took one last look out the back of the aircraft, taking in a deep breath of American air before the pilots got the bird rolling. He hadn't planned on leaving U.S. soil again, but Cal's invitation was too much to resist. This was his family. It was Cal's father, Col. Stokes, who'd given MSgt Trent a second chance. Spurned by the Marine Corps, it was SSI's founder who'd hired him and allowed him to regain his honor. He said his thousandth silent thanks to the man who was probably watching them even now, smiling as they departed to fight together.

Cal, Trent, Daniel and Gaucho. There wasn't a day where they didn't spend time together. Now they were off to war.

Arm in arm. Together. It was humbling for the huge Marine to be with such men, his sense of pride swelling as he prepared himself for what was to come. There were no other people on the planet he would rather shed blood with, possibly die with. Despite his size and strength, Willy Trent cherished sentimentality, never taking his friends for granted. With his heart full, the Marine master sergeant took one more breath of treasured air and turned to join his companions.

As he turned, he caught a set of headlights in the distance out of the corner of his eye. He stopped and squinted. One vehicle morphed into two and then he could make out the small convoy as it neared. Trent walked farther down the ramp and headed out to meet the vehicles. They weren't expecting visitors.

The two lead vehicles peeled left and right, making room for the armored limousine to pull up to where the plane sat waiting.

Trent smiled and strode out to meet their guests as the Secret Service agents did their thing, securing the area and opening the rear passenger door.

President Zimmer stepped out, followed by Travis Haden and Gen. McMillan.

"Well this is a surprise. Isn't it past your bedtime, gentlemen?" asked Trent as he joined up with the three.

"We thought we'd come by and see you off," said the president, shaking Trent's hand. He looked up fondly. "I couldn't send you off in harm's way without saying goodbye."

"The men will like that, Mr. President." Trent nodded to Travis and McMillan. "Why don't we have a little fun with the boys," said Trent, grinning. He led the way into the aircraft, no one paying attention as they walked up the ramp.

"Surprise inspection, ladies. Drop your cocks and grab your socks!" boomed Trent.

The elite team looked up in surprise, half of them coming to an involuntary position of attention.

"You crazy Marines," the president said with a smile, patting Trent on the back, making his way to the rest of the men. By now everyone was on their feet in varying levels of confusion.

"I know you're on your way out, but I wanted to stop by and say good luck," said Zimmer.

"You didn't have to do that," said Cal.

"Yes, I did." Zimmer met the gaze of the international team. "If there's anything I've learned from guys like Cal and Master Sergeant Trent, it's that you guys are the tip of the spear. I have a job because you stick your neck out when the rest of the world is content to sit on their asses."

There were murmurs of agreement, nods and grim smiles.

"I can't overstate this, gentlemen. What you're about to do is vitally important. You all know that. Some of you have seen the enemy in previous tours. This time it's different. You fly off to face the best financed terrorist force in the world. Misguided citizens from around the world defend them and flock to their call. You know the truth.

"I want you to know that I'm behind you, that I'll do anything I can to make sure you come out victorious. You are warriors of the highest caliber, like the Spartan warriors of old. You've come together from across the world, men dedicated to freedom and what is right. Few you may be, but beware the enemy who encounters you on the battlefield. Thank you for your continued sacrifice. Your duty will not be forgotten. Good luck to all of you, and God bless."

President Zimmer moved down the line, shaking each man's hand, looking them in the eye with a personal thank you. Finally, he came to Cal, his friend, the man who'd done the most to open the president's eyes to the dangers of the world and the bravery of its heroes.

"When did you get so eloquent?" asked Cal.

"Lots of practice."

Zimmer shook Cal's hand and looked him straight in the eyes.

"Be careful, Cal."

"I always am."

"Good luck."

Cal nodded and watched Zimmer go. Trent joined his fellow Marine as the president's security force converged and escorted their liege back to his chariot.

"Nice of him to stop by. That's a good friend right there," said Trent.

Cal shook his head. "No, Top. That's a great president."

BAGHDAD, IRAQ

Close to twenty-four hours later, Cal and his international team touched down at Baghdad's airport. They didn't have to play the customs game. Instead, they were ushered to a small convoy of vehicles waiting on the tarmac. A Marine in utilities met them as they made their way off the Globemaster.

"Mr. Stokes?" asked the Marine gunnery sergeant.

"That's me, Gunny."

"Sir, I'm Gunny Mason. We've got vehicles waiting to take you to the embassy."

"What happened to the helos?"

"They were grounded last night. Someone decided to take pot shots at our birds, so the ambassador decided it was safer to drive you there."

Cal could tell by the look on the gunny's face what the Marine thought about the order.

"Lead the way, Gunny."

Once out of the airport, an escort of Iraqi police pulled in front of them and led the way to the embassy. It was a short ride, the roads nearly empty. You could see the heat in the electric haze, making it look like it was foggy out.

At the embassy gate, the Iraqi police peeled off and went on their way. The embassy vehicles never stopped, pulling straight in, the reinforced doors closing behind them, the Marine guards watching them pass.

They parked in front of a row of nondescript buildings, and Gunny Mason led them to their temporary quarters. The plan was to get a couple hours sleep before meeting with the ambassador. He and the CIA station chief were the only ones they'd be dealing with. The ambassador to Iraq was a holdover from the last president, but Zimmer told Cal he was a pretty good guy.

SUNRISE CAME QUICKLY. CAL YAWNED AS HE LOOKED IN THE mirror, opting not to shave. He wasn't trying to impress anyone. If the ambassador didn't like the way he looked, screw him.

Cal and Daniel were the only ones going. The rest of the men had been told to get what rest they could. They'd be leaving later that day.

As the Marine sentry guided them to their meeting, Cal looked around at part of the 104-acre embassy. At a cost of nearly $1 billion dollars, the American embassy was the largest of its kind. Opened in 2009, the exact number of people employed varied depending on who you asked. Cal had heard anywhere between 5,000 and 15,000. He was betting on the larger number just by the size of the place and the amount of workers already heading to their jobs.

Cal had heard the news reports detailing the recall of certain diplomatic personnel in light of ISIS's progress. He knew no fortress was impenetrable, but this one sure looked like it. Patrols, both foot and vehicle mounted, passed them at regular intervals as they walked. Cal knew heads would roll if the new embassy was ever overrun.

They approached the impressive stone structure that looked more like the Pentagon than a diplomatic outpost. The damn thing had to have walls twenty feet thick.

THE MARINE CORPORAL WHO'D PICKED THEM UP FROM their quarters showed them to a private conference room. He said he'd be waiting outside when they were finished. Cal thanked him as he and Daniel stepped inside.

They were early, and yet two men stood to greet them. One Cal recognized immediately from the picture he'd pulled up on Wikipedia on the flight over. Ambassador Luke Brighton had the air of someone who came from money. A career civil servant, the one-time attorney had an easy smile and silver-streaked brown hair. Cal thought he looked like one of those male actors you saw in financial planning commercials, brilliant teeth and perfect hair.

The other man was his polar opposite. Short where Brighton was tall, and nattily dressed in a mussed tan suit, Rich Isnard looked like he'd run life's roughest roads. Although he appeared to be in his late fifties, Cal had learned that the man was only in his early forties. Already a legend at Langley, the recovering chain smoker had come highly recommended by the CIA director. "There are few better than Rich," he'd said.

Ambassador Brighton greeted them with the flourish of a career politician, smiling at Cal like he was a long lost son. Isnard was more reserved, no smile, just penetrating eyes that seemed to take in every bit of the visiting Marines.

They took their seats and Brighton began. "Well, gentlemen, the president had nothing but good things to say about you and your team. While I don't know the specifics of your mission, I hope we can be of assistance."

Cal had at first disagreed with Zimmer's idea of meeting with the American Chief of Mission, but the president had asked for the favor. He wanted Cal to show his face, to the right people, of course. That way, in case there was an incident, there would be more incentive for the CIA and the ambassador to help. Brighton had only been told that Cal's team was in the country on a surveillance mission, to get a better lock on the ISIS threat.

Rich Isnard, on the other hand, knew everything. He'd be a key link for Cal and his men, if Cal chose to use him. According to the CIA director, not only had Isnard's staff developed a network of contacts in and around Baghdad, he also had access to resources throughout the country, having personally spent time in Basra and Mosul prior to taking over in Baghdad. If there was anyone who knew Iraq, it was Isnard.

"Thank you, sir," Cal replied. "Hopefully we won't be needing anything except a few hot meals and a place to stay. I promise we'll keep out of your staff's way."

Brighton nodded. "Good. Now, if one of you can flip the light switch, I'll run you through the current situation. Rich, feel free to chime in."

AN HOUR LATER, CAL SAT BACK AND DIGESTED WHAT Brighton had shown them. It was obvious the man knew his stuff, rattling off locations, names and troop strengths like he'd memorized them the night before. Isnard hadn't interrupted once. He'd opted to listen and watch.

"Any questions, gentlemen?" asked Ambassador Brighton.

"No, sir. Thank you for taking the time to put it together

for us. That gives us a good snapshot of what's going on," said Cal, anxious to get back to his men.

"It was my pleasure. Hell, I feel like I give the same spiel every day." The others laughed dutifully, even Isnard. "Well, if you'll excuse me, I have breakfast with a Jordanian delegation in ten minutes."

Brighton rose from his chair, the others following suit. As he went to grab the doorknob, he turned and said, "Have a safe stay in Iraq, Mr. Stokes," and left the room.

The Marine corporal poked his head in once the ambassador was gone and asked, "Are you ready to head back, sir?"

Cal started to respond, but the CIA station chief spoke first. "I'll take them back, Corporal. We've gotta make a stop on the way."

"Yes, sir. " The Marine nodded and closed the door.

"We can find our way back," said Cal.

Isnard grinned. "What, and miss out on my dime tour? Come on. Let me show you around."

THE CIA MAN WASN'T JOKING. HE LITERALLY GAVE CAL A tour (Daniel left them to brief the rest of the men), showing him the huge Olympic-sized pool, the PX and even the laundry facility. Cal was starting to think the guy was nuts when he took them up to the rooftop of one of the apartment complexes that housed the embassy employees. Cal had things to do and this guy thought they were in Disney World.

Isnard nodded to a pair of Marines that were doing some kind of inspection, looking out over the Tigris, probably half expecting an incoming round. Once they'd made their way back downstairs, Isnard pulled out an electronic cigarette and took his time clicking it on. After taking a long drag, letting out the thin cloud of vapor, he said, "Andy tells me you're a good man."

The comment caught Cal off-guard. "What did you say?"

"Captain Andrews, or should I say Major Andrews, says you're a good man."

Marine Major Bartholomew Andrews, Andy to his friends, had served with Cal in the Marine Corps. Andy had been Cal's platoon commander. They'd fought and almost died together, each earning a Navy Cross for their exploits on the battlefields of Afghanistan and Iraq. The last he'd heard, Andy was at Marine Barracks, 8th & I, leading one of the silent drill platoons.

Cal had honestly been too busy to keep in touch, assuming that his good friend was probably in the same boat.

"When did you see Andy?" asked Cal.

"He came through about a week ago."

"Isn't he still at 8th and I?"

Isnard shook his head. "He's interning with us."

Cal couldn't believe what he was hearing. If anyone was going to be a career Marine, it was Andy. Hell, Cal had tried to recruit Andy no less than five times over the last couple years, but Andy stood firm. He wanted to ride out his time in the Corps, continue to lead Marines.

While part of Cal respected him for it, another more cynical part of the former staff sergeant had often wondered how long the warrior would last in the increasingly bureaucratic confines of the Corps. Andy was one hell of an officer, probably the best Cal had ever served with. He could get a high-paying job anywhere he wanted. A natural leader, the guy just got it. Cal found it hard to believe that Andy was planning on going into the CIA. Why hadn't he called?

"Interning with you? What are you talking about?"

Cal was starting to get pissed. It felt like the spook was toying with him, telling him things he should know but didn't. A game.

"If you're wondering why he didn't tell you, blame me," said Isnard.

"You're not making any sense. How about you get to the point. I've got things to do."

Between puffs of nicotine, Isnard said, "Nice attitude, Marine. You're momma know you're out playing cowboys and Indians?"

Cal almost cold-cocked the guy. He glared at Isnard, and then noticed the grin creeping out from behind the hard eyes.

"What?"

Isnard rolled up his right sleeve and showed Cal his arm. There was a faded Eagle, Globe and Anchor tattooed on the man's forearm.

"Corporal Richard Isnard, USMC at your service, jarhead."

"You prick. I was about to throw you off the roof," said Cal, but he was smiling now. Marines and their off-color sense of humor.

"So you wanna tell me what Andy was doing here?" asked Cal.

"He's on his way to Afghanistan. Keep that under your hat."

"Why did he come through here?"

"Like I was saying, I recruited him. I happened to be at an evening parade at Eight and Eye last year and we got to talking. Not many Navy Cross winners in the Corps, and I was curious. I figured he wasn't one of those pansy-ass officers and he didn't think I was one of those too cool for school James Bond types. One thing led to another and he took me up on my offer."

"Which is...?"

"He's doing some cross-training with us for now, see if he likes it. Still gets to wear the uniform and he can always go back if he wants."

"Is that why you wanted to take us on your little tour?" asked Cal, starting to realize that he liked the natty spook. He could tell the guy was full of piss and vinegar, just like you'd expect from a former Marine corporal.

"I mentioned Andy because I figured it was the only way you'd trust me. My boss's boss said you can be a little...hardheaded."

"You talked to Zimmer?"

Isnard nodded. "I met him when he flew in last month. Found out that despite being a democrat, he's a good guy. We connected the dots and found out that Andy was a mutual friend. He called me a couple days ago, told me to do what I could to help you. I told him I would."

Cal chuckled. "Well hell. Is there anything you don't know about me?"

Isnard shrugged and pocketed his e-cig. "A good spy never digs and tells, Mr. Stokes. Now, tell me how I can help."

It took Cal ten minutes to outline their plan. Isnard asked a couple questions, and made two recommendations. Overall he agreed with Cal, and said he'd pull every string he could to help out.

"When do you make contact with the Israelis?" asked Isnard.

"Tomorrow morning."

"You've got some big balls, Marine. Make sure you're locked and loaded. That area's like the Wild West right now. I'm surprised they picked it."

Cal had thought the same thing, but deferred to his Israeli contacts. The head of Mossad himself had vouched for the men. These were valued agents whom he trusted completely.

"Don't worry. We're ready. What are you gonna tell the ambassador?"

Again, the sly shrug from Isnard. "Brighton's a pretty good guy. Ivy Leaguer, but not a total snob. He knows why I'm here and pretty much stays out of my way. He gets that the president's keeping him in the dark on this. It's probably better for him anyway."

"Why's that?"

"Would you rather tell the Iraqi president truthfully that you have no idea what's going on in his country, or lie right to his face?"

"Good point. So, tell me about—"

Their conversation was interrupted by three explosions spaced narrowly apart. By the sound, the three men knew they weren't close by.

"Mortars," said Cal.

Isnard nodded, looking out over the landscape along the Tigris River. "There." He pointed. Three thin plumes of dust and smoke were rising from what looked to the riverside edge of the embassy compound.

"Does this happen a lot?" asked Cal, not really surprised by the incoming rounds. They were in Baghdad after all.

"Not much anymore. The Iraqis—"

Three more explosions sounded, this time inside the embassy compound. It didn't look like anything had been hit, but sirens started wailing. Then, as if on cue, a loud roar erupted from the north end of the embassy, like a stadium full of football fans cheering for their team, or wailing in dismay.

Isnard spun around to where the cheer had come from. "What the—?"

The explosion knocked them from their feet. They could hear screams from the street, probably wounded. Cal's ears were ringing. He looked at Isnard, who'd scraped his elbow in the fall, blood seeping from the tattered hole in his tan suit.

"Let's get you back to your team," said Isnard, already leading the way.

"What the hell's going on?" asked Cal, not necessarily worried, more curious at not knowing the daily rigors faced by the embassy staff. He figured the explosions were fairly routine.

Without looking back, Isnard said, "We're under attack."

BAGHDAD, IRAQ

The Iraqi colonel picked up the four well-used olive drab seabags and tossed them in the trunk of his car. Twenty million U.S. dollars. He'd be wealthy, minus the promised payments for his subordinates, but they probably wouldn't be alive to see it. They didn't know that, and that was fine with the colonel.

Passed over for a promotion for almost ten years, his time had come. While his peers gazed down from their lofty positions, he was stuck doing administrative tasks fit for a new recruit. Like today. He'd been assigned to oversee the military parade showcasing Iraq's beefed up arsenal. Like the days under Saddam, the Iraqi government wanted to show the world that they were, in fact, a viable ruling force.

They wanted ISIS to see their strength, the weapons that would soon drive them from Iraq. Stupid. Instead of attacking, they were parading.

ISIS had contacted him through his sister's cousin, a radical sympathizer who'd listened to the colonel's drunken lamentation weeks before. The seeds planted carefully, the colonel recognized the casual courting immediately. He'd taken small payments and favors in the past, but this was different. There was no going back to his old life. There would be a helicopter waiting to take him and his family to Syria and then out of the Middle East.

"The ammunition is loaded, Colonel," said one of his captains, the man who would stay behind and coordinate the attack. The colonel had promised him half a million dollars. Not a king's ransom, but enough to start a new life for the bachelor.

"Very well. You know your target. The signal will be three mortar blasts. Keep up the barrage until the Americans send in their air support. Then, you and the other commanders may proceed to the designated rendezvous point for extraction out of the country."

The captain smiled. "Yes, sir."

He did a precise about face and marched off toward the waiting vehicles.

If he were a religious man, the colonel might have said a short prayer for his men. But he wasn't. Instead, he got in the back of his car, told his driver where to go and dreamed of where his newfound riches would take him.

* * *

7:21AM

Martin Gleason beamed. His many months of hard work had paid off. There were almost fifteen thousand Iraqis crowded into the southeast corner of Al Zawra Park. Many carried Iraqi flags. There were smiles and hugs between friends, a coming together for a common cause.

Gleason was an American who'd left his high-paying

corporate job in Manhattan to come to Iraq, to change the country desperately in need of peace. It was his mission in life, his dream. He'd met roadblocks for the last three years. Corrupt officials. Constant military presence. Apathetic citizens. Slowly he'd built his reputation, helping the needy, painting a picture for a beautiful new Iraq. An Iraq without war.

The government official he'd had to pay off thought they were marching north, headed northeast towards Sadr City. But that wasn't what Gleason had planned. The peace march would begin at the park and proceed southeast on 14th of July Street, passing the embassies of the United Kingdom and the United States. Gleason relished the thought of seeing the war mongers looking down, marveling at his handiwork. Countries like Iraq didn't have peace rallies; they had strikes and mobs. Gleason's event would be a first.

Sure, he'd had to pay a lot of people to show up, but that was the price of mass mobilization. It would be worth it. *Time* magazine was doing a piece on the march that would coincide with the large military parade moving north. Other media outlets promised to send reporters and help chronicle the historic event. No one knew they were on a collision path with the military parade. All except Gleason. Again, he'd planned it that way.

There was sure to be a confrontation, but Gleason hoped for it. He relished the thought of peaceful demonstrators going up against the ruthless military. By this time tomorrow there would be pictures of his victorious masses all over the world. His staff had already prepped their social media presence for the inevitable swell of support.

They were minutes from starting their slow walk. He picked up his megaphone from the ground and switched it on. It was time to prep his marchers.

Just as he lifted the device toward his lips, a hand grabbed

his arm. Gleason looked back, thinking it was one of his assistants. It wasn't. The man holding his arm was dressed like the
rest of his supporters, but the stern look in his eyes belied his
intent. Gleason stared wide-eyed, now noticing four others
standing behind the man.

"Do not say anything," said the man in Arabic, taking the
megaphone out of Gleason's trembling hand. "If you do, you
will be shot."

The man nodded to his companions, who disappeared
into the crowd.

"What do you want?" asked Gleason. He could feel his
bowels shifting. He'd been robbed three times since coming
to Iraq. Every time he'd pissed his pants. It felt like he was
about to do it again.

"We want the same as you, Mr. Gleason."

For a split second, Gleason relaxed, hoping that he'd been
mistaken about the stranger's motives.

"You do?"

"Yes, Mr. Gleason. We want to show the world something
they've never seen."

The man depressed the button that blared the siren out
of the megaphone, silencing the happy crowd. Then
he spoke.

"By order of the caliph, and under the blessed gaze of
Allah, this demonstration is now under our watchful eye. Do
not call out or try to run. We have men placed throughout
your gathering. Obey and you will live, earning the everlasting
gratitude of the caliph. Run and you will be shot. Gather your
belongings, we leave in two minutes."

Gleason stared at the man in horror. What was
happening?

* * *

8:03AM

The military procession moved out from the staging area. A company of two-hundred Iraqi soldiers led the way, stern-faced and fluid with their heels clicking against the pavement.

Next came ten Russian-made BM-21s with truck mounted 122mm multiple rocket launchers. Behind them were five M109A6 Paladin howitzers. Firing a 155mm shell, ISIS had recently captured close to twenty of the American-made self propelled artillery weapons.

Finally came the columns of armored personnel carriers, an assortment of Russian, American, British and even Chinese manufactured vehicles. Some boasted machine guns of varying sizes, bored troops manning them as they rolled slowly down the road.

Crowds dotted the sides of the road, mostly curious, not really there for the event. They'd had enough of military parades under Saddam. In those days Iraqis were required to attend such events. At least now they could come and go as they pleased.

The procession moved along Two Stories Bridge, around the Jamia Street roundabout and north toward the U.S. Embassy. Although the sparse crowds couldn't see it, fingers were starting to hover over triggers and buttons inside the vehicles.

* * *

8:06AM

EgyptAir Flight 637 was almost empty. Five customers were scattered throughout the aircraft, cared for by three flight attendants. Sometimes there were too many passengers to bring into Baghdad. It depended on the season and the political climate. With the continued movement of ISIS, passengers were scarce. It didn't matter to the crew. They were getting paid whether they had a full compliment or two passengers on the Boeing 767 aircraft. In fact, they'd been promised a bonus to man the flight for a week at a time. A fifty percent pay raise was pretty good for a short hop.

They were waiting for final clearance to descend into Baghdad's airspace when the harsh buzz from the secure cockpit door sounded. The pilot looked up in annoyance. The rear crew knew not to disturb them right before landing, especially coming into the city. There was always the off-chance that some budding terrorist wanted to shoot them out of the sky, and the two pilots had to be ready.

"Go see what they want," the pilot ordered his second-in-command.

The co-pilot got up and went to the door, looking through the small bulletproof glass window. It was the stewardess, a pretty girl in her mid-twenties who'd been making eyes at the captain all morning. She was new and the co-pilot was pretty sure she had an IQ below what was acceptable for airline duty.

The girl, Jamila, smiled and motioned to the back of the plane. She'd probably forgotten the rules. The co-pilot exhaled and opened the door.

"What is it, Jamila?" he asked.

She put her finger to her lips, eyes still playful.

"What is it?" the co-pilot asked again, ready to close the door in the stupid woman's face.

Jamila smiled and raised her other hand to chest level so only he could see. It held a small caliber pistol with a suppressor on the end. It was pointed straight at him.

"Turn around and walk back into the cockpit," she said, her eyes no longer playful, now dark and menacing.

The co-pilot nodded, his mouth suddenly dry. He was a

veteran of the Egyptian army, had been to war and seen men die. But something in Jamila's eyes spoke of doom, the focus of a fanatic.

He turned around, Jamila stepping in and closing the door behind them. The co-pilot never felt the bullet that blew through his left temple, through his brain, and out the right side of his head.

* * *

8:13AM

The three teams uncovered the 81mm mortars secured in the back of their three battered pickup trucks. They knew there was little time. The American counter battery units would lock on to them quickly. Two shots, maybe three. They'd agreed to move to the next location after two.

Honed from hours of practice, the first mortar dropped into its tube and flew north, its companions dropping and flying a second and third a few seconds later. They waited for the distant explosions, shifted north a degree, and then let loose the second volley.

As soon as the fourth, fifth and sixth rounds were in the air, the crews scrambled back into the vehicles and sped off to their next firing point.

* * *

8:14AM

Gleason could barely walk. His legs shook with every step. His supporters, proponents for peace, moved along reluctantly. They'd seen the men with guns hidden under their clothing, casual with their gait but firm in manner. No one had been shot yet and Gleason hoped it would stay that way. As long as everyone listened.

They'd made it to the gates of the U.S. embassy, the walls looking down at them, cameras watching their every move.

The siren on Gleason's megaphone sounded, and the ISIS commander's voice boomed.

"By Allah's name, cry out to Him if you want to live. Tell the infidels they do not command you!"

The first cry sounded from close by, soon spreading. Gleason's voice joined the thousands in a desperate cry that sounded more like a wail.

* * *

8:15AM

At the sound of the exploding mortars, the military procession stopped. The marching troops halted and looked across the Tigris in confusion, some bringing their rifles to the ready. The vehicles behind them stopped, engines still growling. But there was no confusion in the minds of the gunners.

Turrets and barrels shifted left. A small child in the crowd next to the road pointed at the swiveling weapons. Without warning every missile launcher, howitzer and vehicle-mounted machine gun started firing at the U.S. Embassy. The sound was deafening to the ears of the onlookers. As the firing continued, the crowd ran.

* * *

8:16AM

Jamila looked at the pilot's lifeless body and grinned. He and the co-pilot had taken her for a fool, assuming she was a stupid woman. She was not.

The caliph had picked her personally from their growing female ranks. She'd been specially trained for this mission. The glory would be hers.

She pulled a small remote out of her pocket, twisting the power knob to ON and depressing the red button. The airplane shook slightly from the small explosion on the left wing where she'd hidden the incendiary. It wouldn't hinder the airplane's flying ability, but it would buy her time.

Jamila picked up the radio and spoke to the control tower as she carefully guided the plane into a steep descent.

"Baghdad, this is EgyptAir six-thirty-seven, we have experienced some kind of malfunction, possibly an incoming round on our port wing. We are losing altitude quickly."

"Copy, EgyptAir. Be advised, we have reports of fighting in the city center. Do not, I repeat, do not fly over the city."

"I'm not sure that's possible. Our controls are unstable and—"

Jamila took off the headset and threw it on the ground. The news of fighting was good. Her brothers had struck the first blow.

As she looked down at the smoke now rising from the middle of Baghdad, she increased her angle of descent, aiming the nose of the plane at the outpost of the infidel, the American embassy.

BAGHDAD, IRAQ

8:15AM AST, AUGUST 15TH

Lieutenant Commander Dillon McKay, call sign "Crapshoot," looked out of the cockpit of his Navy F/A-18/E Super Hornet. He'd been on station for ten minutes, just the routine stuff they did every day. Intel hadn't said anything about imminent threats, so the fact that he was watching the center of Baghdad implode was surreal.

He'd called in the situation. They told him to stay close, that nobody knew what was happening on the ground. *Those ISIS bastards caught us by surprise*, thought McKay, a twelve year naval officer who'd recently left his wife and two kids for another seven-month deployment. His little girl was about to start kindergarten and he was going to miss it.

McKay dropped farther out the clear sky, his wingman close behind.

"Let's get in close," he said to his fellow pilot, a short Italian from the Bronx named Joey Nitalli, call sign "Herringbone" for the expensive suits he loved to wear when he was off duty.

"Take a look at that firepower."

McKay watched as streams of missiles reached out and tagged the American Embassy, one after another.

"Are those mobile howitzers?" asked Nitalli. They were still too high to see every detail.

"I think so. Paladins maybe. Higher needs to hurry up and give us the go-ahead."

As they made their way to the deck, still waiting for word from higher, something flickered in McKay's peripheral vision. He turned his head.

"Jeez. Is that a 767?" he asked, more to himself than his wingman.

Nitalli was saying something, but McKay didn't hear. He was switching to the civilian air frequency. The air traffic controller was hollering in Arabic.

"Baghdad, this is U.S. Navy 212. We have your aircraft in sight. What's the situation?"

The air traffic controller was in a frenzy. He switched to accented English. "Navy, we have lost contact with EgyptAir. They reported a malfunction—"

"They're heading straight toward embassy row, Baghdad."

The controller swore, screaming something to someone else in the tower. "I cannot be sure, Navy, but we think the plane has been hijacked."

McKay swore under his breath. If they were going to do something they had to do it now. He had seconds to make a decision. If they shot it with their missiles, who knew where the aircraft wreckage would go. The carnage could be worse than a direct hit by the airliner.

He did the quick math in his head, the time as one of the elite Blue Angels flooding back suddenly. An omen. Hundreds of hours of flying wing to wing, nose to tail. Precision flying. Some of the scariest stuff he'd ever done, but it might help him now. He made his decision.

"I've got this, Herringbone," he said, now talking to his wingman again.

"You can't shoot that thing, man. It'll—"

"I'm not shooting it."

McKay made a hard left and came around to shadow the falling 767. He had no idea if his plan would work, but he had to try.

"What are you—"

"Stay back, Joey. Tell my wife I love her. Crapshoot, out."

He switched off the radio to avoid Nitalli's objections. His multimillion dollar jet could easily outrun the 767, but all he needed to do was catch up. McKay touched the picture of his wife and kids taped to the control panel, and said goodbye.

* * *

8:17AM

Cal and the CIA station chief were taking steps four at a time, running past scared embassy staffers until they finally got outside. It was pure chaos. Explosions all over the huge compound. Cal thought it was bad, until he looked up.

He could plainly see a civilian aircraft flying toward them, flying in from the west, in a steep angled descent. Cal grabbed Isnard's arm and pointed up.

"What the—" said Isnard.

"Run!" yelled Cal, sprinting away from where he predicted the aircraft would hit. Not that they'd have much of a chance, but he'd be damned if he just stood there staring up at the sky like some others were doing. Frozen in shock.

As he looked over his shoulder, he noticed another aircraft close to the airliner. Possibly American. For a split second he wondered why they weren't shooting the thing down, but then it hit him. It didn't matter. Even if they did, it would still land on the embassy. So what was the other plane doing?

* * *

8:17AM

Jamila was surprised that she hadn't been shot at. She could just make out people scrambling on the ground. Infidels realizing their death neared. Most were still focused to the east, where her brothers continued the dual diversion. She relished the thought as she came in slow, wanting her enemy to see their peril when it snuffed them out.

For some reason she looked left, and for a moment she thought she was dreaming. There was a military jet closing in, maneuvering close. She could see the pilot's outline, obviously looking straight at her.

It didn't matter. There was nothing the fool could do. The caliph had planned it that way. If they blew up her plane, the same thing would happen. Tons of twisted metal, fuel and consuming fire engulfing the American embassy.

Jamila turned away from the jet that she could now see was American by its markings. Good. The man would have a front row seat to his people's death.

She gripped the controls harder and focused straight ahead, anxious to be part of the killing below.

* * *

8:18AM

Cal and Rich Isnard made it to the only decent shelter they could find, a grouping of huge concrete barriers waiting to be placed somewhere else. It wouldn't help them when the plane crashed down, but they had to go somewhere.

Done running, the Marines looked up, watching as the pilot of the F-18 saddled up next to the civilian plane.

"What's he doing?" asked Isnard.

"I don't—"

As they watched, the F-18 flipped onto its side so the top of the cockpit was now facing the larger aircraft. The world slowed, the F-18 and 767 touched. Cal couldn't believe what he was seeing. In the motion picture in his brain, Cal saw the excruciatingly slow momentum of the larger plane. It was like having a front row seat to inevitable ruin. Dreamlike.

Cal lost the view a split second later, when an explosion sent him flying.

BAGHDAD, IRAQ

Lieutenant Joey Nitalli, call sign "Herringbone," watched wide-eyed as his wing man, and good friend, somehow did the impossible. Honed from years of some of the best flying Nitalli had ever seen, McKay altered the 767's path, its downward trajectory painfully slow.

To an untrained eye it would have seemed that the F-18 was having no effect, but Nitalli saw it, the shift as they plunged through the seconds, the falling feet. McKay's fighter was like a sheep dog herding a charging bull, subtle pressure applied expertly. Nitalli counted it down in his head. *Three, two, one.*

The interlocked aircraft narrowly missed the southern wall of the embassy complex, plunging spectacularly into the Tigris River. Water shot every which way like the footstep of a titan, drenching a wide swath of the coastline.

Nitalli said a silent thanks to his friend, the man who'd saved his career. No one else would've gone to bat for him, telling the admiral that he'd take care of the free-spirited Italian-American. McKay said he believed in the hotshot, and took him under his wing, literally and figuratively.

Back in the present, the squadron was chattering in his ears, but he didn't hear it. He knew they were coming to help, still precious minutes out. He willed away the tears that blurred his vision. There would be time to mourn later. A proper tribute.

There was something he could do. A quick look at the ground and he found his target, the military parade that was still firing round after round into the American Embassy.

Screw the rules. It was time for payback.

* * *

8:20AM

The Iraqi captain knew it was almost time to leave. No forces had engaged them yet except for the stray round from the embassy. The Iraqi government had been very clear on any use of military force within the city. In fact, they'd helped the Americans craft rules of engagement that were even now precluding them from firing into civilian neighborhoods.

But that would change. He'd watched the American fighter pull off the miraculous save, the sound of the crash still ringing in his ears.

Just as he reached for the radio to order their withdrawal, he saw something flash overhead. Another plane, fast, probably American. No payload dropped.

Good. I have time.

He ordered his fellow traitors to exit their vehicles and retreat to their rendezvous point. As the last word left his lips, the two lead vehicles in the column exploded, flipping one and sending the other spinning into a building where it crumpled into a fiery heap. The captain knew what was coming before it hit. He heard the clank, but never felt the explosion of the AGM-65 Maverick air-to-surface tactical missile that sent him to hell.

* * *

8:22AM

Ambassador Brighton's hand shook as he waited for the president to come on the line. No stranger to war-torn lands, the blatant attack on the seemingly impenetrable embassy shocked the veteran public servant.

"You there, Luke?" asked President Zimmer, a hint of alarm in his voice.

"Yes, sir."

"Tell me what you know."

"Sir, just after zero-eight-hundred Baghdad time, explosions, we think mortars, began the attack on the embassy. Not long after, from south of our position, a military procession started a rocket and high caliber round barrage. At almost the exact same moment, a crowd of demonstrators, estimates say between ten and twenty thousand Iraqis, attempted to overwhelm our main gate." Brighton paused, wiping the sweat from his forehead with a soaked handkerchief.

"Go on."

"We're still piecing the rest together, sir, but we believe there was also an attempt to crash a commercial airliner into the complex."

"How is that possible? Don't we have that airspace buttoned up?"

"I don't know, sir. We're putting it together as best we can." The Marines were the ones who kept sending runners to the deep bunker, breathlessly handing the American ambassador sheets of handwritten paper with their commander's assessment. It was chaos overhead.

"Do you know where Stokes is?"

Brighton almost said, "Who?" before he remembered the man he'd met not hours before. "No, sir. I saw him earlier today, and then he left with Mr. Isnard."

"Okay. Hang tight, Luke. We're sending help."

The line went dead and Brighton looked up as another runner entered the secure room.

"Sir, the mob just broke through the first barrier."

* * *

8:25AM

Cal came-to slowly, aware that he was laying on something soft. Grass? He took a painful breath as his eyes fluttered open. Isnard was ten feet away, not moving.

"Rich," croaked Cal, his throat dry. No movement from Isnard.

Cal tested his arms and legs, grimacing when he felt the fresh pain. It didn't feel like anything was broken and he didn't see any blood. Lucky. Just banged up. He couldn't remember what had thrown them, probably an explosion.

Then the whole scene that had played out overhead came screaming back. If he was breathing, at least the planes hadn't crashed into the compound. Cal felt a buzzing in his pocket and thought that maybe his leg was spasming. He touched his thigh and realized it was the phone in his pocket.

Cal answered the call.

"Stokes."

"Cal, it's Brandon. Are you okay?"

"As far as I can tell." Cal could now see Isnard moving, struggling to get to his hands and knees.

"I just talked to Brighton. He told me about the demonstrators and the rockets. What about the EgyptAir jet?"

Cal didn't have a clue what Zimmer meant about the demonstrators. Then he remembered the sound he'd heard before, the roar of a crowd.

"I didn't see where any of it came from. I felt it. All I saw was that brave bastard who saved everyone."

"What are you talking about?" asked Zimmer.

Cal told him about the F-18 and what the pilot had done.

"I've never seen anything like that in my life," said Cal, still amazed. "You better give that guy the Medal of Honor if he really did what I think he did."

Zimmer grunted. "I'll take care of it. What about—"

Like the charging cavalry, Cal saw Daniel Briggs leading his column of international warriors around the corner not thirty feet away, running toward the main gate. Cal shouted to get their attention.

Daniel turned his head, and the men headed toward Cal and the bloodied CIA station chief.

"Cal, you still there?" asked Zimmer.

"Yeah, sorry. Look, I've gotta go. I'll call when I know more."

"Okay. Be careful."

"Sure."

Cal placed the phone back in his pocket, gratefully taking Daniel's hand, and was pulled to his feet. Everyone crowded around, weapons bristling. No one looked afraid, eyes steeled for battle.

"What took you guys so long?" asked Cal.

"We came as soon as we could. Didn't know where to find you," said Daniel, handing Cal his FN MK20 assault rifle and extra magazines. "What happened?"

Cal gave his men a rundown of what he knew. No one

flinched, digesting the news like the seasoned warriors they were.

"Let's find the Marines and see how we can help. Rich, you okay to show us the way?" asked Cal.

Isnard nodded, his scalp above his left ear oozing blood. He had another wound under his right eye. "Yeah. Let's go."

Without another word, they trotted toward the sounds of ongoing battle, into the mouth of chaos.

U.S. EMBASSY

Master Gunnery Sergeant Mark Morris had spent the last twenty-two years of his life in one Marine Corps post or another. After enlisting in the Marines at the age of eighteen and serving his first tour as a 0311 (infantryman), Morris volunteered for MSG (Marine Security Guard) duty. He wanted to see the world and figured embassy duty was the best way to do it.

A meritoriously promoted corporal and sergeant, the clean cut Texan was a perfect fit for MSG. He'd been on embassy duty off and on since, serving all over the world.

This was supposed to be his last tour, a promise to his wife. She'd been pissed he'd wanted to go to Iraq of all places. He'd assured her that the enormous embassy in Baghdad was a fortress that couldn't be breached.

He was eating those words now. While he wasn't ultimately responsible for the security of the entire embassy, the Marine in Morris took it personally. This was *his* embassy.

He was standing on the roof of the highest building in the complex, giving him the best vantage point. But it also made him a perfect target. Luckily, the walls he kept peeking over were reinforced with enough metal and concrete to stop anything but the highest grade explosives. And not that the bastards hadn't tried. The vehicles south of the river had slammed them with rockets and high caliber rounds, wounding three of his Marines already. His boys were still mobile, each taking a quick bandaging and going back to their duties.

The situation on the ground was chaotic, but it wasn't anything compared to the airplane that had almost taken them out. Morris saw it all, how that crazy air jockey had somehow pushed the larger aircraft into the Tigris. CMH for sure for that brave bastard. Thousands of lives saved.

While the normal staffers ran to secure locations, the operators working for the embassy, and even those just passing through, had run to the sound of battle. It was Morris's job to help coordinate the defense and possible counterattack. He'd already had more than one heated conversation with American military commanders who'd cited Baghdad's rules of engagement (ROEs) as a reason for not sending in artillery and close air support.

Luckily, whoever the pilot was flying the second Navy F-18, he took out the BM-21's and paladins pounding from across the river. With that group taken care of, and the civilian jet at the bottom of the river, what was left, other than the occasional mortar round, was the screaming crowd trying to get through the gate.

The last Marine he'd sent to get a better look, a new kid from Cali, had never come back. He was about to send another scout when the door of the stairwell emptying out onto the roof slammed open. Armed men streamed out, the lead guy coming straight toward Morris. The others fanned out, trying to get a better view of the surrounding area. Some looked like foreigners.

"Master Guns?" asked the man. Young face, but cool eyes. He carried one of those 7.62 rifles that SEALs loved. FN-something.

"How can I help you?" asked Morris, not really in the mood to brief strangers. He was busy.

"A fellow Marine sent me."

"Who's that?"

"Rich Isnard."

Morris's eyebrow rose. Most people thought the CIA station was a prick, but Morris liked the guy. In fact, the two Marines had hit it off from the beginning, even getting together occasionally to take money from the senior embassy staff who thought they could swindle a couple of grunts over a few games of Texas Hold 'Em. They'd become friends. If Isnard sent this guy, he probably liked him, *and* he was a Marine. Good enough for Morris.

"How can I help, Mr.—"

"Stokes. Actually, I wanted to see what we could do to help you."

Morris thought about it for a moment, another mortar round exploding a building away. He noted that none of Stokes's men flinched. Pros.

"The shacks at the main gate were overrun. I don't have a clue what's going on. I've already lost one Marine and was about to send more to see."

Stokes nodded. "We'll take care of it."

The grim smile on the man's face made Morris curious. He'd never seen the guy before. "Can I ask what you guys are doing in Iraq?"

The smile widened. "I could, but then I'd have to kill you."

Morris nodded, returning the smile despite the dire situa-

tion. "Good luck, sir. Oh, and take this." Morris handed
Stokes a handheld radio.

Stokes nodded and walked to where he could better see in
the direction of the front gate. He said something to a man
carrying a M40 sniper rifle, the preferred weapon of Marine
snipers. The guy with the blond pony tail nodded and
gestured back to Morris. They exchanged a few more words
and the man looked at the master gunnery sergeant again,
throwing him an amused wink.

I'd bet my next paycheck that guy's a Marine too, thought
Morris. It almost made him laugh. For some reason, despite
the smoke and mayhem, Morris breathed a little bit easier as
Stokes and his men rushed down the stairwell. He'd have to
buy those guys a round at the club if they made it back alive.

U.S. EMBASSY

They had to get a good view of the mob. Impossible from the inside. If they scaled the walls, there was the very real likelihood of being shot. The screams were deafening as they approached the main gate. Mortar rounds had taken out chunks of pavement and pieces of the protective nine foot blast walls. Dead bodies littered the way, staffers who'd died in the initial barrage. Cal didn't see any dead Marines.

Daniel pointed to an oversized construction excavator up ahead, its tilting bucket now lying on the ground.

"Maybe we can get a better look with that," he said as they ran.

"You know how to use one?" asked Cal.

"I'm sure one of the others do."

They got to the Caterpillar brand excavator.

"Anyone know how to work this thing?" Cal asked the rest of the team.

Valko raised his hand. "I can."

"Good. Me and Daniel are gonna take a look. Don't drop us, okay?"

Valko nodded and made his way to the vehicle's cab. Apparently the keys were still in the ignition because the Bulgarian cranked it up immediately, maneuvering the arm around so that the front of the cab now faced the high wall.

Cal and Daniel hopped into the bucket and were lifted into the air. They had decent cover behind the metal plating unless someone had an RPG, Cal figured. The tracked vehicle shifted into gear and moved forward, its arm extending out and up, reaching.

They could see over the first wall and then the second. Arms waving, some members of the mob were carrying flags.

"They don't look like terrorists," said Cal, scanning the crowd as they lifted into a better vantage point, careful not to expose themselves too far from behind the clawed bucket.

Daniel had a pair of mini binoculars to his eyes.

"I don't see any weapons," said the sniper.

"What? How is that possible?" Cal had never faced down a group this large. The crowd extended back as far as he could see, easily filling the street abutting the embassy.

Daniel didn't answer for a moment, and then pointed suddenly. "There's a guy with an AK." The sniper unslung his rifle and took a look through his scope. "I could take him out, but...Cal, the rest of those people look scared."

Cal grabbed Daniel's binoculars and panned over the screaming crowd. Everything came into focus when he saw the tear-streaked face of a woman carrying a wailing child in her arms. "What the—?"

A round pinged off the thick bucket, making both of the Marines duck.

"I don't think this is what we thought it was," said Cal as he motioned for Valko to lower them down to the ground.

"Me neither," agreed Daniel.

The leaders of the international teams gathered around when they touched down.

"What's the situation?" asked Gene Kreyling, the Brit obviously ready to do something productive.

Cal shook his head. "I can't be sure, but this doesn't look like a mob that wants to storm the embassy."

"They already overwhelmed the first layer of defense," argued Owen Fox, the Aussie's wavy hair held back by a red bandana.

"I think we've got agitators in the crowd, probably prodding the rest. The worst thing we can do is start firing at innocents," said Cal, trying to figure out how they could deal with the situation.

No one said a word. It was one thing to kill an enemy. It was quite another to find them like a needle in a haystack and kill them without wounding everyone else.

The initiative was taken from them as the first head popped over the wall, the man throwing his arm and then leg over. He was not armed, eyes wide as he took his first look into the complex.

"Fox, take your snipers to the best vantage point you can get. We may need your cover. Daniel, you go with them. The rest of us will split into two teams and hop over the wall. Maybe we can get around the crowd and find out who's pulling the strings."

There were no objections, their options limited. Already there were more embassy security forces sprinting to the main gate. They could take care of the people climbing over. Cal had to find whoever was controlling the thousands just outside the embassy walls.

Less than five minutes later, Cal's half of the team, which included MSgt Trent, the Bulgarians and the Japanese, scaled the wall at a point where they'd determined the crowd couldn't see them.

The Japanese went over first, assisted by thin but sturdy black line with grapple hooks that snapped open with a click.

Cal couldn't believe how fast Kokubu and his men went up and over. Nimble ninjas. Cal, Trent and the Bulgarians went next, not as swiftly, but successfully.

Cars littered the road, drivers having decided it was better to leave them where they were rather than getting caught in the ongoing battle. The team spread out and trotted toward the crowd. In less than a block the mob came into view.

The crowd's attention was on the embassy gate, giving Cal the ability to get his team in close. Apart from the yelling and lack of weapons, nothing seemed out of place.

A moment later Cal heard a distinctive rifle shot in the distance. It had to be the snipers. One down and who knew how many left to go.

The crowd pulsed with agitated energy, surged forward and back as if willing the front row through the heavily rein-forced embassy walls. As they neared, one man turned around, his face hard, concentrating. His eyes bulged when he saw Cal's men, his arm lifting from under his robes, a sawed-off shotgun rising in hasty aim. Cal and Valko were the first ones to respond, easily putting three rounds apiece center mass, the man going down before he could pull the trigger.

"Let's split off in twos. Valko, you're with me," said Cal.

The Bulgarian didn't argue.

Cal assumed the ring leaders were probably on the periphery just like the guy they'd just shot. It would make it easier to find them and kill them. Sure enough, not thirty seconds later, another weapon popped out. Cal disposed of the shooter with a clean shot in the face.

The next guy jumped on Valko from behind, but the strong Bulgarian flipped the man over his body, crashing into scared onlookers who backed away as much as they could in the cramped crowd. Valko didn't hesitate, crushing the man's face with three powerful strikes from the butt of his assault rifle.

Three more shots from Daniel and the Aussie snipers. Good, but not good enough. Cal was starting to think it could take forever to find the rest of the enemy when Kokubu walked up holding a katana blade, its razor sharp edge lined with blood.

"We saw armed men running away from the crowd and found the demonstration organizer. He's American," said Kokubu, in his matter-of-fact tone. Cal couldn't believe the guy was holding a sword. There'd be time to ask about that later.

"Where is he?"

Kokubu pointed back over his shoulder.

CAL FOUND THE AMERICAN SITTING ON THE STREET, HIS pants soaked, probably with his own urine. He was shaking as he tried to gulp water from the canteen one of Kokubu's men had given him.

"You okay?" asked Cal.

The man, who looked like a prototypical Ivy League bookworm, shielded his eyes from the sun with his free hand.

"Who are you?" he asked.

Cal ignored the question. "Tell us what happened."

The trembling man told them the story, including how they'd been ushered at gunpoint toward the embassy and how one of his assistants had been shot for refusing to scale the wall.

"I mean, they just shot him, right there in front of me. This was a peace march for God's sake!"

He was crying as he cradled the canteen to his chest.

"Where did they go?" asked Cal, who was nervous standing out in the open. The others were covering him, but he was still a sitting duck.

"The shots started a couple minutes ago, and the guy in charge heard something over his earpiece. They took off right after that."

"How was he communicating with the crowd?"

The man pointed to something lying on the ground a few feet away. Cal saw the megaphone and went to pick it up. It was cracked from where someone had dropped it on the ground, but it still came to life when he switched it on.

He held the thing out to the guy on the ground.

"I need you to tell them that it's over."

* * *

Somehow there weren't many wounded peace marchers. Most were scared and more than happy to disperse when Martin Gleason, the march organizer, told them it was okay to go home. Cal directed Gleason to tell them to take their time leaving so no one would get trampled.

Whether because of tired relief, or the thought that guns were still trained on them, the crowd broke up gradually. Friends huddled together, crying as they held each other close.

The wounded were triaged by the Japanese while the dead bodies of the ISIS soldiers were left for someone else to clean up.

Cal knew they'd been lucky. It could've been a lot worse. His team had come away unscathed, but they were all as ready as Cal to go on the offensive. They left the cleanup to the embassy security personnel and the Iraqi police. Cal and his men slipped through the throngs and made their way back inside the embassy.

THE WHITE HOUSE

President Zimmer stood behind the curtain and waited for his cue to take the podium. By now everyone had heard about the attack on the embassy in Baghdad. Few people knew all the details. The president was one of a handful.

Hours before, ISIS had posted a video lauding their brave soldiers who'd stormed the embassy, killing thousands of Americans in the process. It was a lie, a way to save face and try to get ahead of the global media. Zimmer would not let that happen. It was time.

"Ladies and gentlemen, the president," announced Bob Lundgren, the White House press secretary.

Everyone in the packed room stood as Zimmer marched in. There were whispers as they noticed his attire. No shirt and tie. No suit or even a sport coat. He wore a leather bomber jacket with *President B. Zimmer* embroidered over the right pocket and a patch over the left that had the words *United States* embroidered on the American flag. It had been a gift from a group of special ops vets the month before. They'd invited him to Tampa for a roundtable discussion about the ongoing terrorist threats. Though no longer part of the active duty military, those men still felt deeply responsible for the future of their country and the free world. They'd offered to help. He hoped those men were watching now. Warriors like them had inspired him to act.

"Thank you all for coming. I'd like to address the American people first." Zimmer looked directly into the camera, his eyes determined, lips tight. "Fellow Americans, as most of you know by now, at approximately one o'clock in the morning Eastern Time, the terrorists of ISIS attacked our embassy in Iraq. We don't have the complete picture yet, but I can give you what we do know. The number of dead and wounded is still being assessed.

"At 7:15am Baghdad time, a group of approximately fifteen thousand unarmed marchers, dedicated to pursuing peace in Iraq and the Middle East, were accosted by armed ISIS thugs. The peaceful marchers were herded to the gates of the U.S. Embassy as a diversionary tactic. Ten were killed and over one hundred were wounded.

"The second diversion came from south of the embassy where an Iraqi military parade was commandeered by traitors within the Iraqi army. Countless rockets and artillery rounds pounded the embassy complex as embassy staffers started their day. Dead and wounded littered the embassy streets as the cowards assaulted from across the Tigris.

"While the two diversions engaged from the north and south, an EgyptAir 767 was hijacked by another ISIS element. The hijackers took control of the plane and aimed for the heart of our embassy. The embassy currently employs over ten thousand Americans and foreign nationals, most of whom were on their way to work."

Zimmer paused, his eyes softening as he began again.

"Were it not for the selfless and heroic action of Navy Lieutenant Commander Dillon McKay, a husband and father of two, a former member of the Blue Angels, who somehow guided the larger airliner out of its intended path and into the Tigris River, thousands would have been lost. Fittingly, McKay's call sign, Crapshoot, given to him for his steadfast belief in doing the right thing despite the possible outcome, served his purpose. It could have gone either way, but due to his skill and ultimate sacrifice, the aerial attack was thwarted.

"I have spoken to Lieutenant Commander McKay's wife, Patty, and extended my condolences along with the gratitude of the American people. Because of the number of witnesses to McKay's act, along with the bi-partisan support of Congress and the unanimous support of our military leadership, Lieutenant Commander Dillon McKay will receive the Medal of Honor posthumously at a date determined by Mrs. McKay.

"Commander McKay wasn't the only hero in Baghdad. His wingman, Lieutenant Joey Nitalli, a second generation Italian-American from the Bronx, took the initiative and wiped out the entire column of vehicles that continued to pound our embassy with deadly fire. Unopposed, those vehicles would surely have killed many more were it not for Nitalli's bravery. I commend him for his actions and have recommended to the chairman of the joint chiefs that Lieutenant Nitalli receive the Navy Cross for his actions.

"Despite what some of you may think, these are not dark times. The bravery of our men and women in and out of uniform shows us there is always hope. No matter how close the peril and no matter how deep the opposing evil, we will stand, heads held high, jaw set, united.

"That brings me to the next part of my address. To the thugs and prospective recruits of the group known as ISIS, your time has come. While you may think the American people are weary of war, I am here to tell you that her military is not. You see us as a weak country that would rather lounge on the beach than fight. You couldn't be more wrong. What you've forgotten is that in addition to our armed forces, we also have thousands of former special operations veterans who've come to me personally and volunteered for future service. They, along with our active duty military, can't wait to come find you.

"Effective immediately, my administration will do everything in its power to protect the American people *and* its allies. This is not a question of money or power. This is a battle between right and wrong, between good and evil. We will win. This will not be a fight; this will be a tsunami overwhelming your forces wherever they might be.

"To the American people who believe that war is wrong, that peace should prevail, I would say that I agree. But in order to have peace, we must first have justice. We cannot and will not negotiate with terrorists or their supporters. These murderers will not see a courtroom and they will not see the inside of a jail cell. There is only one fate these cowards deserve.

"Here is my six step process for how we will first start with ISIS and then build an international force that will fight terrorism and corruption wherever it appears.

"First, in dedication to Lieutenant Commander McKay, Operation Crapshoot commenced at six o'clock this morning. I've directed a handpicked team currently deployed in Iraq to coordinate a tenfold increase in aerial bombing and close air support. In addition to aerial support, fifteen civilian security companies, including delegations from our international allies, are flying special operations veterans into Iraq. Those forces will be tasked with finding and annihilating ISIS, wherever they walk, eat or sleep. I've been told that they can't wait to get started.

"Second, going forward, our military will be a major component in our battle against evil. Militaries need training. I've been assured by General McMillan and his staff that there is no better final training test than live combat. So without much more expenditure, we will do two things, train our troops of the future, and wipe out international threats.

"Third, I have a message for our allies. If you need us, we will be there. If evil raises its ugly head, we will be with you, arm in arm, fighting for what is right. But that aid comes with a caveat. Our allies must be dedicated to the common global ideals of personal and religious freedom. Any supposed ally who ignores these terms will find themselves without impunity. A criminal is a criminal. A thief is a thief. Decide which side you're on, because our side carries a big stick.

"Fourth, to the religious leaders of the world, especially those of Islam, though we live with differing traditions, we are still one people on this Earth. What one person does always has the possibility of affecting others. If you want to be part of our community, it is time to do your part. Denounce the criminals who besmirch your faith. Tell your followers the true meaning of the Koran. Do not let the money and influence of hypocrites taint your religion or your people. We request that you do this now, respectfully, or face the scrutiny of America and our allies.

"Fifth, starting today, an unprecedented coalition of three former American presidents, my predecessor included, will travel around the globe to strengthen our alliances. Much like our brave military leaders, we will lead from the front, go where we are needed. We will go toe to toe with any who would seek to undermine our good intentions, and who trample the freedoms of our citizens. In the coming days you will find out how great our resolve truly is.

"Sixth, my staff is in the process of drafting a proposal for the members of the United Nations. The proposal will outline our recommendations for the formation of an international terrorism strike force along with an international tax that will fund ongoing anti-terrorism operations. Only the countries that contribute to this fund will be supported by the strike force. You pay to play."

Zimmer's eyes lightened, a smile appeared where moments before a scowl stood firm.

"To the citizens of the world, I tell you that help is coming. Stand with us. Raise your voices for good. Do what is right, not what is convenient. Help your neighbors. Do unto others as you would have done unto you."

The president's voice trailed off. The only sound in the hot room was the clicking of pictures and whirring of video cameras.

"So there it is. You're either with us or against us. Choose wisely, for as President Teddy Roosevelt once said, *It is only through labor and painful effort, by grim energy and resolute courage, that we move on to better things.* Thank you for your time, and may God bless you all."

President Zimmer turned and walked off stage, the roar of the reporters' questions following him out.

MOSUL, IRAQ

I t was almost two hours after the American president's address that The Master got to see it. The power had been out most of the day along with his internet connection. No doubt the Americans were somehow involved.

He watched Zimmer's address three times, silent, listening to the man who'd so abruptly taken over the helm of leadership in the land the caliph considered his greatest enemy. The man formerly known as Kiril Valko digested the news without blinking. For months he'd tried to get an indication of what Zimmer's response might be, what kind of man he was. It wasn't until today that he got a true sense of Zimmer's agenda, a glimpse into his soul. Always careful in his planning, Kiril knew ISIS had overstepped. He had planned poorly.

Every detail of the Bagdad operation had been planned with simplicity in mind. He'd learned that years ago when first commanding a group of illiterate peasants who couldn't read a map, let alone follow a set of complex orders.

Overwhelming force virtually guaranteed their success, but cruel fate stepped in. If the attack on the embassy had gone as planned, nothing else would have mattered. The Americans could bomb them until their dollars were spent and he could care less. It was supposed to be the key to decades of future recruitment around the world, much like the attacks on 9/11. Videos of the death and destruction could be used for years to come. Outposts and strongholds built. Armies raised.

Unfortunately, the Americans had gotten lucky, thwarted his brave warriors and the Iraqi army officers who he'd paid handsomely. Even now the Iraqi colonel tasked with the military parade diversion was being tortured, soon to be within an inch of his life. He'd hidden the millions somewhere, but the interrogator told The Master that the information would soon come. After all, they had the rest of the colonel's family watching their patriarch, waiting for their turn in the blood drenched cell.

Kiril clicked his laptop closed and inhaled deeply. The reports were coming in from across Iraq and Syria. The Americans and their allies were bombing his brothers, many scurrying for hiding like cowards. If he wasn't careful, his troops could be decimated. Although he believed those killed would live happy in the afterlife, he couldn't let it happen. He needed his men if his plan was to succeed.

Establishing the caliphate in the Middle East was important, vitally so, but there were still other things to accomplish. Kiril Valko, Bulgarian by birth but a faithful follower of Allah by reawakening, stood from his chair, raising his hands to the ceiling, eyes cast to the heavens. *Guide me in my quest.*

* * *

ERBIL, IRAQ - KURDISTAN REGIONAL CAPITAL - 4:57PM AST, AUGUST 15TH

Hasan al-Mawsil marveled at the level of advancement in the Kurdish capital. He'd been there many times over the years, each trip finding that many things had changed. In the decade since Saddam's ouster, a huge influx of international aid, primary American, flowed into the Kurdish stronghold. New buildings rose into the sky on what seemed like a daily basis. Shopping centers and office building housed international corporations that saw the Kurds as valuable allies.

Erbil was prospering despite the infighting in Baghdad and the encroachment of ISIS. The city of 1.5 million residents stood strong against the horde, one of the few bright spots in a tangled web of Iraqi inconsistency and bickering.

Hasan sat in the ancient Citadel of Erbil overlooking the rest of Erbil from its 100-foot plateau. Shaped in a rough circle, the original heart of the city looked like a shallow bowl from the sky. Some said the citadel was the oldest continuously inhabited town in the world. Hasan had heard that only one family remained in residence while the old fort was renovated, cranes and trucks dotting the streets at regular intervals. There was deep history in its stones. Hasan could feel it.

He felt a million miles away from Mosul even though the distance was just over fifty miles. A short drive.

His contacts said the Americans would meet him soon, probably under the cover of darkness, as was their way. It couldn't happen soon enough.

He'd watched the American president's address with a mixture of excitement and fear. Hasan knew that if the Americans wanted to do something, they would do it. Their warriors were said to be the best in the world. He'd met many Americans over the years. Most were courteous and humble, people Hasan could respect. Brave like his brother. Who else would fight far from home, death likely every day, all for the freedom of a foreign land?

There were still hours until the appointed time, and Hasan allowed himself to relax for the first time in months, gazing out over the city, waiting for the sunset, and the Americans.

* * *

IRAQ HAD EXPERIENCED IT BEFORE, THE MIGHT OF THE American military, the relentless bombings, the deep thrumming of tremulous explosions. They'd been warned to lay low, allow the attacks to commence, not get in the way. Even now the distant booms from cruise missiles and drone attacks could be heard intermittently. It was beginning.

It would be worse when darkness fell, the invisible specters of high altitude bombers and swooping aircraft dropping their pinpoint payloads. Death dealers in the night.

Much had changed since 2003, but many things had not. The ancient system of cronyism and bribery resurfaced despite the best efforts of America and its allies. It was too entrenched from centuries of corruption. Every day its dark tentacles reached out to ensnare more willing servants. No one was safe, least of all the politicians hidden safely in their compounds, lording over the masses.

But now the American president was saying he would deal with these tainted men, those who sought to suppress freedoms, not just in Iraq, but around the world. It was too hard to believe, that one man could do such a thing. How could he dare it? Would he succeed?

No one knew the American president, this Zimmer, but they were about to find out about his resolve. Iraqis would experience a night filled with the screams of the dying, the last gasps of jihadists, the silence of the dead. The ISIS Passover had begun.

OUTSKIRTS OF MOSUL, IRAQ

2:19AM AST, AUGUST 16TH

Not a light in the sky. Clouds blanketed the area, portending doom. The air was heavy, like something had sucked out the oxygen and replaced it with a lingering breathless fog. These were good things for the small troop moving swiftly through the night. Not a word was said.

Hasan al-Mawsil stopped mid-stride, peering into the darkness with the night vision goggles the American had given him. His breathing measured, Hasan pointed with the index finger of his right hand like the compass of fate directing dark angels to their target.

Still without speaking, the American and his team left Hasan where he stood, fanning out in the night. Soon they were gone from his sight. He sat on a rock and waited, his job finished for the time being.

* * *

THE TINY VILLAGE, TEN CRUDE HOMES SITUATED IN A

rough L pattern, came into view moments later. Daniel had taken point. None of the others argued, each understanding the Marine sniper's uncanny ability to sniff out danger and point unerringly toward the enemy.

He heard a dog bark in the distance, followed by a loud yelp. Probably a kick from its master. It didn't come from the village, but farther north, maybe a click away. Noise carried in the desert.

Daniel filed the thought away as he released his grip, allowed himself to slip into the killer, the beast whose primal urges clawed to the surface. He'd tamed it over the years, released it only when needed. Daniel suppressed a growl when he saw the first signs of movement ahead.

Guard, came the thought in his head. Without thinking, he signaled to the men behind him as he unslung the sniper rifle from his back and replaced it with his assault rifle.

Silent as death, only the light scraping of boots on the hard packed earth, the Brits pushed past Daniel. They would breach the perimeter, followed by Cal and the Bulgarians. Daniel and the Aussies would provide overwatch from afar while the rest of the team moved in to support the raid.

A silenced round spat twice, followed by the falling body of the ISIS guard hitting the ground. Daniel moved off to find more prey, the beast eager, panting for blood.

* * *

GENE KREYLING CHECKED TO MAKE SURE THE MAN HE'D shot was dead, then followed his man Rango further into the village. A second later, Tango Number Two fell to the ground, three silenced rounds in the face from Rango's weapon.

The guy from Mosul, Hasan, said there were twelve to fifteen ISIS men hunkered down in the small outpost. ISIS was supposedly using it as a processing station, sifting through the trucks carrying confiscated valuables and weapons on their way to an unidentified location. Hasan thought maybe this was where they were caching weapons for their army.

Kreyling wasn't taking any chances. In his experience, if a native said twelve to fifteen, you best prepare for at least double that number.

A drunken shout came from one of the huts. Kreyling went that way, feeling Stokes and the others close behind. He heard the faint sound of three more guards taken down before he got to where the shout had come from. Had to be the Japanese. Those boys were good.

The shout repeated, this time more urgent, annoyed. Kreyling didn't speak Arabic, but figured it was probably the commander calling out for his guards. He guessed he had maybe a minute before the man came out of the dimly lit doorway and actually did his job.

The British team of three stacked just outside the wooden portal, Kreyling in the lead. *Three, two, one.*

Kreyling smashed through the brittle wood, quickly entering the twelve by twelve space. A surprised half-naked fundamentalist looked up from where he was mid-thrust into the backside of a naked girl. There were two more watching, both sitting against the wall.

The observers had weapons. They died first, barely having time to get their hands off their crotches and reach for their triggers. Kreyling leveled his weapon at the open-mouthed ISIS commander.

"Go to hell," growled the Brit as two bullets left his weapon and took the man in the throat, his head lolling to the side weirdly as he fell to the ground, blood gushing from the wounds.

With his two men guarding the entrance, Kreyling approached the girl cautiously. She looked shell-shocked, a single tear running from her blank eyes. Who knew how long they'd had their way with her. *Bastards*. The poor thing reminding the Brit of his own daughter, a fifteen year old spitting image of his ex-wife.

He lowered his weapon as she backed away, doing little to cover her exposed form.

"It's okay," he said, picking up a discarded blanket from the floor and handing it to her. For the first time, life flickered in the girl's eyes as she grabbed the offered cover and brought it against her body.

Kreyling grabbed the flickering gas lantern from the ground and gave it to the girl. He saw bloodlines running down her exposed legs. His mind raged. This was why he'd come, why he'd left an easy job of ferrying rich businessmen around the world. There was absolute evil on this planet, ISIS being one of the many culprits. The innocent trampled by the whims of power hungry zealots who masked their ambition with religion.

"I'll be right back," he said, pulled by the sound of Arabic shouts from outside. The girl could wait.

Kreyling put his finger to his lips, and motioned for the girl to stay where she was. She nodded mutely, wrapping more of the blanket around her body.

"Let's go, boys," said Kreyling, eager to send more of the bastards to their final resting place.

* * *

THERE'D BEEN FIFTEEN MEN MANNING THE ISIS OUTPOST. They were all dead. No casualties for Cal's team, just a couple of dings that Kokubu was attending to.

"That hut was stacked full of weapons," said MSgt Trent, who'd just returned from inspecting the village with Gaucho.

"All kinds of stuff, boss," said Gaucho. "AKs, M-16's, even some HKs and Barretts. Ammunition is in the hut next to it."

"Did you get video of everything? Faces too?" asked Cal. One of the things he wanted to make sure they had was proof of the guys ISIS was recruiting. They needed to know where they were coming from. A few snapshots and some video would give them what they needed. Neil would do the rest.

"I did," answered Trent.

"Good. Moretti, can you take care of the weapons?" asked Cal. They'd brought enough explosives to dispose of any cache they couldn't carry out.

The Italian nodded. "Give me five minutes."

Cal looked at his watch. The helos would be there in just under ten minutes. One raid down, one more left before daylight. The Marine wanted to get as many missions completed before ISIS got wind of what was going on. With their army being pounded day and night by the international coalition, it was only a matter of time before ISIS either ran or made their last stand. Cal hoped they were stupid enough to fight back.

WEST OF MOSUL, IRAQ

3:41AM AST, AUGUST 16TH

A den Essa was beginning to regret his decision to follow his schoolmates to Iraq. Three weeks earlier, the twenty-year-old Egyptian was enrolled at Al-Azhar University in Cairo. He'd studied business under the insistence of his father, and was less than a year from graduating. Once Aden completed his degree, he would be first in line to take over the family business, a small electronics company housed in a dingy third floor box in Cairo.

He hated the place, even though his proud father had spent years building it. To Aden, the shop represented all that was wrong with the Arabic world. The toil of hardworking Arabs who would never see the riches they so desperately deserved.

Aden envisioned a utopia, a land where Islam flourished after the defeat of the infidels. A place where goods and services were shared amongst brothers. No one would be hungry. No one would be without a home.

His college friends believed in the dream as well, and

they'd watched banned ISIS videos on a university computer owned by the president of the university himself. The old crab had never installed proper security measures in his office or on his computer. It was an easy feat for the innovative young men to break into the room. Should the use ever be detected, it would be the head of the university who would be implicated.

Ever since ISIS moved into Iraq, the five friends had plotted their escape. ISIS was looking for warriors, men who would see the Word of Allah spread to every corner of the globe. Aden Essa wanted to be such a man. A hero to millions.

But now, driving the lead vehicle in a five truck convoy laden with toddlers and pre-teen boys, Aden's doubt grew. He'd seen things. Terrible things. While it was one thing to watch a beheading on a computer, it was quite another to witness it first hand, to clean up the slimy blood from floors and walls. To smell the bowel waste and sour piss of dying men, women and children.

He wasn't a warrior; he was one of hundreds, if not thousands, of janitors tasked with cleaning up the ISIS's carnage. The first two times he'd vomited, violently. The older men had laughed at him along with two of his friends. The second time he'd thrown up in his sleep, memories of the smell still in his nose as he dreamt of the massacre reaped hours before.

Like a sailor gaining his sea legs, the smell and sight of devastation no longer unfurled his stomach. But his mind was not numb. He recognized the unholy and this was it.

Aden wondered what his mother and father would think if they knew he was driving a truck full of young boys to pleasure the perverted whims of supposedly holy ISIS warriors, only to be butchered when they were through. He pictured his younger brother, Rashad, who was only twelve years of age. Just like the boys in the back of the truck. The thought made him nauseous.

As he refocused on the dark road ahead, his headlights doing little to cut into the drooping blackness, Aden felt a jolt as the truck's engine suddenly gave out. He slowly applied the brakes as steam and smoke rushed out of the hood of the vehicle, hanging lazily in the still air.

He checked his side mirrors and saw to his relief that the others had slowed as well. He'd seen more than one driver rear-end another by following too closely. None of those illiterate peasants knew how to drive.

Aden climbed out of the cab and waved to the man driving the next truck in line.

"Engine!" he yelled.

The man nodded and put his vehicle in park. Aden could hear the old gears creaking as the convoy settled in to wait. Hopefully the others wouldn't just sit there.

The young Egyptian didn't know much about vehicles other than the quick classes the gruff ISIS logistics man had taught them. How to add fluids. How to change tires. But Aden knew nothing about fixing an engine. They were supposed to be in good working condition.

With some effort, he popped the hood open, smoke billowing in his face. He immediately worried that the vehicle would explode, but then remembered his father saying that such things only happened in movies. His father knew about automobiles.

Trying to sweep the smoke away with his hand, Aden never felt the .50-caliber round that tore his body in half.

* * *

THE AMBUSH WORKED TO PERFECTION. ONCE THE LEAD

vehicle was stopped by a well-placed round from Daniel's Barrett, the convoy was a target ripe for the taking.

It didn't take long for Cal's concealed forces to dispatch the drivers and secure the vehicles. There were no guards, just untrained drivers.

MSgt Trent signaled the all clear. Front and rear guards posted without a word. The huge Marine grabbed the high handle on the back of the first truck and stepped up to bed level. He clicked on the red light on his vest, illuminating the cargo.

He estimated close to fifty boys of varying ages packed in. Scared. Trembling.

Trent hadn't wanted to believe what Hasan had told them before stepping off. The Iraqi had somehow caught wind of the shipment from friends inside ISIS, men who were risking their lives to gain valuable intelligence for the resistance. Hasan was one of few middle men privy to the information. Trent gathered that the man from Mosul had a wide web of informants. He would have loved to know how that came to be.

"You're safe," said Trent. Some of the boys must have understood English because the whimpering started, then an exhale of relief flooded the compartment.

TAL AFAR, IRAQ

F or two days the assault leveled heavy casualties on his forces. In broad daylight and under the cover of darkness. The attacks never relented.

What first started as a trickle soon became a full blown leak of ISIS recruits fleeing the battle zone. Even when they ran, the Americans and their allies pounded them with bombs, riddled them with bullets and cut their throats with fine blades.

Weeks before, ISIS was the ravaging army, slicing its way across the Middle East. Now it was the international coalition, led by the Americans, who'd become the lurking shadows, death around every corner.

The Master digested it all. The whispered stories amongst even his most faithful followers spread like the plague. To make matters worse, the destruction was not contained to the battlefield. The hundreds of millions of dollars the leaders of ISIS had deposited with banks around the world either disappeared or were seized by the host country. It was an unprece-dented move by the international community. Even his fellow Arabs were joining the hunt. He'd become the prey.

More detrimental was the nearly closed recruiting pipe-line they'd so carefully fostered. Social media and a strong internet presence had allowed them to touch fundamentalists around the world, to rally them to the caliphate. Since the American president's declaration, those sites were now in the hands of the Americans. Multiple times throughout each day new videos were posted. Not videos he'd crafted, but ones taken and produced by the Americans. Footage of his holy warriors killed in every way possible: sniper fire, machine guns, bombs, missiles and even blades.

The message to potential recruits was clear: *Join ISIS and we will kill you*.

His normally serene facade showed signs of breaking. Face caked in dust, robes torn and splattered with dried blood, The Master looked more like a vagrant than the leader of an anointed army.

Earlier in the day he'd ordered a score of captured deserters to die by firing squad. It was the only way to main-tain control and discipline. His ears still rang from the event that was held in an abandoned gas station instead of outdoors. He couldn't take the chance of being seen by drones and satellites.

Movement was impossible. Darkness didn't help. The infi-dels' technology negated any benefit night might bring. The Master did not like limited options. He liked remaining static even less.

They had him on his heels, struggling to maintain control of his forces. Luckily, ISIS commanders had enjoyed a decen-tralized command structure since their invasion of Iraq. They had The Master's orders, and were trusted to carry them out as they saw fit. Failure would not be tolerated. And yet, failure seemed an inevitable conclusion.

The Master said a prayer, raising his hands in humble tribute, seeking the answers he so desperately needed.

* * *

ERBIL, IRAQ - 7:20PM

They hadn't stopped since the attack on the American embassy days before. The team snagged rest when they could, but even the most battle-hardened were starting to feel the strain. For that reason, Stokes had ordered a respite in the Kurdish city of Erbil. They'd flown in on American Chinooks, the trails of smoke plumes rising from the ground behind them.

For Stojan Valko, the endless raids had come as a welcome distraction. To the Bulgarian, idle time was not time well spent. Ever since his childhood, he'd had a hard time sitting still, staying in one place.

But now he allowed himself to relax if even for the briefest moment, standing on the roof of the boutique hotel where they'd commandeered the top two floors. He gazed out over the city, amazed that its citizens went about their day despite the war being waged just outside their walls. He knew it would be much different in Bulgaria, as it would be in most other civilized countries.

But this was not his homeland. It was land that had seen bloodletting for centuries. Its people numb to violence, even when it lived next door. The warrior in him knew that unless Iraq's leaders rallied together for a common cause, they would always be vulnerable to threats like ISIS.

While it disturbed the proud man to see a people so easily cowed by terrorists, he relished the idea of being on the other side, of having the ability to kick jihadists back into their filthy holes. To kill them with his bare hands. Valko knew it was a fight he was willing to wage until his last breath, until his heart no longer beat its steady rhythm.

"You gonna get some sleep?" asked a voice behind him. It was Cal Stokes.

Valko did not shift his gaze.

"Soon," he answered.

Part of him did not want to speak with the American. He felt too vulnerable, too close to his raw emotions. It was one thing to plan an attack with the young leader. That was business. It was quite another to be alone with the man, the one who'd given him the second chance.

Valko was not stupid. He knew what the others had thought, and he didn't blame them. Had it been another member who'd revealed his relation to a terrorist, Valko would have been the first to ask for his dismissal.

Thanks to the American, that hadn't happened. Yes, Stokes had kept him close, but he had not hovered, hadn't micromanaged Valko's actions. It didn't take long for the Bulgarian to realize that Stokes was a good man, an honest man, a born leader. Not only had he led by example, always from the front, but he'd harnessed the strengths of each individual, somehow weaving together a powerful group of alpha males who were not used to taking orders. And all without the bravado of the leaders Valko had always looked up to. He had a gift.

It was a hard lesson to learn, but the actions of his new comrades could not be ignored. They'd completed their missions with precision, without harming innocent bystanders. Ruthless in the attack, the men also ushered the kidnapped Iraqis with care, always offering a smile or lending a helping hand.

Valko hadn't known such duality was possible. His career

was built on the warrior's code, putting mission above all else. He'd never cared about the innocents really, always focused on the demise of his enemy. Let the doctors and nurses care for the others. That was how he'd always thought.

And now he found himself questioning, trying to figure out why he was that way. The only answer he could come up with was his brother, Kiril.

Somehow he knew his brother was still alive. It was the bond of twins, forever linked by some invisible thread. He'd never questioned it as a child, always assuming that other brothers felt the same. But they didn't.

Over the years he'd felt his brother even though thousands of miles separated them. Sometimes he would feel a sudden stab of fear, for no reason at all. Other times it was a gush of pride warming his body even though he was doing something mundane like watching television. He knew what it was. It was Kiril. Kiril off becoming a stranger, becoming his enemy. He often wondered if his brother felt the same sensations. He probably did.

Valko never told anyone about their connection, especially after the revelation concerning his brother's conversion. The Bulgarian wondered what it would feel like when Kiril died, when the last shred of air left his body.

"How's Levski feeling?" asked Stokes. Valko had almost forgotten he was still there.

"Better. Kokubu stitched and gave medicine." Georgi had taken a nasty fall in the last raid when he slipped over a concertina topped fence. The bloody gash on his arm would leave an impressive scar.

"Good," said Stokes.

The two men stood watching the city's nighttime routine, Valko not knowing what to say, and Stokes once again respecting Valko's privacy.

"Okay. I'm gonna get a couple hours of rest. Enjoy the view," said Cal, turning to go.

Before he knew what he was doing, Valko turned and said, "Thank you."

Stokes stopped and looked back at him. Valko was a man of few words, not one to show emotion or gratitude. He wanted to thank the American for what he'd done, for trusting him when the others wouldn't. He wanted to ask how he'd come to be the way he was, deadly as a viper and yet as caring as a treasured friend.

Luckily, he didn't have to say anything. The Bulgarian could see by the look in the American's eyes that he understood, that he knew that Valko's simple thanks was more powerful than a heartfelt declaration from most other men.

Stokes smiled, nodded, and went on his way.

Valko turned back to the city, wondering where his altered life would now lead.

LONDON HEATHROW AIRPORT

LONDON, ENGLAND - 2:33PM, AUGUST 24TH

James Cornet rushed to find a restroom. Weeks of eating foreign food had taken its toll. An hour didn't go by that he didn't break out in a cold sweat, bowels rumbling. The flight from Amsterdam was torture. Multiple trips to relieve himself and still no relief.

The first men's bathroom he came to was closed for cleaning. Trickles of sweat were already pooling on his lower back like hanging lemmings. Luckily, he'd worn a black t-shirt. Cornet had learned that lesson on his way into the Middle East. More times than not your body betrayed your intentions. Wear a black t-shirt.

The next restroom was open, and he rushed to get the nearest stall. He barely got his pants down before the deluge commenced. Gripping the handicap handrail on the side of the stall, Cornet barely registered the door to the next stall opening and closing.

He heard the sound of gas being passed, and the audible sigh of relief from his new neighbor. Putting the other man out of his mind, he prayed for perhaps the hundredth time that day that Allah do something to settle his stomach. His father was expecting him, a small gathering of family sure to be there too. The returning hero with a case of the runs. Now that was a story for the ages.

Feeling somewhat normal for the moment, Cornet pulled out his cell phone and checked for messages. None. He exhaled in relief.

His departure from Syria had been abrupt, but less so than the day he'd left Iraq. Loud bombs and silent death from the shadows contrasted to induce outright panic. Cornet was glad he'd made it out in time. So many of his fellow holy warriors had not. Luckily, as a British national, he was able to board a flight first to Istanbul, then Amsterdam and finally home to London.

A knocking on the side of the stall shook him from his thoughts. It must be the man sitting next to him.

"Yes?" Cornet asked.

"You wouldn't mind handing me a bit of paper, would you? Seems the roll is out on my side," said the man in heavily accented Welsh.

It was good to hear the familiar dialect. Cornet had struggled to pick up Arabic. The writing was even worse. English was, after all, his first language, despite his Islamic faith.

"No problem," he said, pulling out a length of toilet paper and rolling it around his hand until he had what he thought would be enough for the man to use. "Here you go."

Cornet reached under the wall to give the stranger the toilet paper. As soon as his wrist passed under the metal barrier, he felt an iron grip clamp down on his hand. He tried to pull away, tugging with all his strength.

It didn't help. With a terrible yank, his head slammed into the stall, stunning him. Seconds later, he realized he was lying on his back, staring up at a man with a gray eye patch.

"Welcome homes, James," said the man, who Cornet now realized was holding a silenced pistol in his other hand.

"What do you—"

"Say hello to Allah, you bloody traitor."

Time slowed. Cornet looked into the calmly furious eye of his attacker, and then into the extended barrel of the gun. He barely had time to hear the muted report of the weapon before two rounds pierced his forehead and cut off his response.

* * *

GENE KREYLING WIPED HIS BOOT ON THE DEAD MAN'S shirt and opened the stall door. Rango poked his head around the corner.

"All good?" he asked.

"Right."

Rango's head disappeared and Kreyling walked to the sink to wash his hands. Four men dressed as janitors streamed in behind him, wordlessly setting to the task of cleaning up the bloody stall.

Kreyling dried his hands and nodded to the men who were placing the terrorist's body in a wheeled hamper, piling trash bags on top.

Another burly janitor stood casually next to Rango as Kreyling exited.

"Let's go. Stokes will want to know that we got our third."

Rango nodded and followed his boss toward Baggage Claim. Three for three. Not bad for their first day back.

* * *

ZENICA, BOSNIA & HERZEGOVINA - 4:29PM

The small Islamic council listened to Daris Gudelj's tale. He'd left months before with five more hand-picked young men who'd proved themselves to the secret fanatical sect of Islam. It was important to send their future leaders off to war, to test their mettle and strengthen their faith. Each of the six elders had spent their youth on treks to Lebanon, Palestine and Indonesia. It was part of their ritual, the path of a man.

And now, out of the six hopefuls they'd sent to fight in Iraq alongside ISIS, only one had returned. The once hand-some Bosnian now looked shattered, shell shocked, a portion of the man he'd once been. Fear now replaced the hope and longing he'd left with.

They didn't say it, but each of the six elders feared what it meant for their community. If word spread, their followers might falter. They'd been careful. Always outwardly friendly to their Christian neighbors. For nearly five decades they grew. Now numbering close to five hundred members, the close-knit community was tight-lipped and autonomous to all but Allah.

That was one of the reasons young Daris sat before them now. He had not been allowed to see his parents. This was his first stop. A decision must be made. While none of the men considered Daris a coward, the implications of his home-coming were obvious. He was tainted. They'd miscalculated. Something would have to be done.

"Daris, tell us again about your return trip. You are certain you were not followed?" asked one of the elders.

Daris nodded respectfully, his hands trembling. "Just as you told me. I spent close to a day in the Balkans just to make sure."

"Good. Good."

Silence once more as the men deliberated.

A buzzer sounded and one of the council members stood. It was his establishment. A single story shop where he sold pastries. "I apologize, brothers. I was not expecting a delivery."

The others nodded absently, too focused on the matter at hand.

A couple minutes later, a tall dark haired man dressed in the light blue uniform of a local delivery company walked into the back room carrying a cardboard box.

"Who are you?" asked the head of the council, annoyed that the shop owner had let the man in.

"Pardone. Delivery. The signore told me to bring it back to you. A small snack for your gathering, maybe?" the man said in what the council leader thought sounded like an Italian accent. There was a growing Italian population on the other side of town. He'd heard they were refugees from the ongoing mafia wars in southern Italy.

"Fine. Put it on the table," said the head of the council.

The delivery man smiled and set the large box on the table. He left without saying another word.

* * *

STEFANO MORETTI LEFT THE STOLEN DELIVERY VAN WHERE he'd parked it across the street from the bakery. He whistled a tune as he walked, his steps light, his eyes focused ahead.

When he was one hundred yards away, Moretti turned around and sat on a low stone wall facing the building he'd left moments before. He extracted his cell phone and tapped the screen. To any passerby the tall Italian looked like one more person fiddling with their phone. A split second later the pastry shop shot skyward in a thunderous boom. The powerful explosives he'd packed under the authentic Italian pastries (his grandmother's secret recipe) worked to perfection.

Moretti knew from experience there would be no survivors. There would be no witnesses except him. A moment later a car pulled up to the curb and he got in as he put his phone to his ear.

"Yes, my friend. The pastries were a big hit."

The small sedan tore down the narrow street as sirens wailed in the distance.

* * *

PARQUE NATURAL SIERRA DE MARIA-LOS VELEZ –- ALMERIA PROVINCE, SPAIN - 9:10AM, AUGUST 17TH

Eduardo Ladicia sped along the park's dirt road. It was lined with forest pine trees that welcomed him home, tall sentinels standing in reverence. The smell of the pine and the fresh Spanish air coursed through his body, cleansing his soul.

His best friend Hugo rode beside him, equally entranced by the ride. They were home after months away. Gone were the boys they'd been before leaving. Now they were men. Battle tested. Stomachs of stone. The courage of lions.

The dirt bikes were the only mementos they'd brought back. Stolen from a youth hostel just outside Adana, Turkey, the two men in their mid-twenties continued their adventurous journey home. Some nights they slept under the stars. Others they begged for a warm pile of hay in a barn.

They'd made it across the Mediterranean in a modest fishing boat, helping the captain and his sons in exchange for food and a ticket home.

Eduardo was glad to be home. He'd seen and done things that still brought terrors in the night, jolting him awake, hands clenched, heart racing.

As he sped along the empty stretch of road, all the memories seemed to wash away, leaving his heart light once again.

They stopped at a small rise overlooking the valley below, their motorcycles purring as if to say they wanted to keep going forever. Eduardo smiled at his friend.

"Almost home," he said.

Hugo nodded. "Yes, it will be good to—"

The coming words were shattered by a loud crack followed by an endless red. Eduardo almost fell back off his bike, just managing to reset his foot. His face felt wet.

"What...?" he looked down at his dust stained t-shirt that was now covered in crimson. His heart raced as he looked back at his friend. Hugo was no longer sitting astride his motorcycle.

The bike lay on its side, its rider toppled over, half a bloody head oozing life onto the dirt and rocks beneath it.

In a split second Eduardo's mind flashed *SNIPER*, and he went to gun his motor, but the round of the .50-cal Barrett sniper rifle was too fast. It tore through Eduardo's body like a scythe through a stalk of hay.

* * *

OWEN FOX TOOK HIS TIME STOWING HIS NEW WEAPON. HIS fellow Aussies swept the area for any signs of their passing. By the time they left, no one would know they'd been there.

Fox dusted off a blade of grass from the barrel of the high caliber weapon as it went back in its case. In less than a month since he'd acquired the American-made weapon from Cal Stokes, the Australian sniper had ninety two confirmed kills.

The ex-surfer smiled as he set his prized weapon in the back of the open-top jeep. It was time to head back for a well-earned beer to the hotel where they were staying.

SOFIA AIRPORT

SOFIA, BULGARIA - 6:43PM, AUGUST 18TH

Much of Cal's responsibility had now been passed to other private operators setting up in theatre. He and his men had been the tip of the spear, but their follow-ons were the ones who were now tasked with the ongoing game of terrorist whack-a-mole.

After leaving Iraq, Cal's men had chased fleeing ISIS troops across the Middle East and Europe. They were killed in airports, taxis and in their hometowns. Now that Neil and the CIA were coordinating with sister agencies around the world, it was almost easy to track down the recruits who'd run to ISIS's rally call.

Cal knew they'd missed more, but he hoped word was still spreading. Neil was in the process of putting the finishing touches on a video compilation depicting the deaths of foreign fighters. It would go live at midnight, posted in all the usual places that wannabe jihadists trolled online.

The president and Cal were in complete agreement as to

the message: *It doesn't matter where you are or where you hide, we will find you and kill you.*

CAL AND DANIEL STEPPED OFF THE AIRPLANE AND MADE their way down the long gangway. Stojan Valko and his men were waiting at the ticket counter.

The former rivals shook hands, the respect between them apparent. They'd run through fire and lead together. In a bizarre string of events, they'd become brothers-in-arms.

"Welcome to my country," said Valko.

"Thanks for the invitation," said Cal. He'd been anxious to get home and take a much-needed week off, but he couldn't ignore Valko's invitation. It had surprised him, and once again proven that warriors, men of proud hearts and limitless courage, could rise above petty misunderstandings and come to respect one another.

The plan was to meet the heads of the Bulgarian government on behalf of President Zimmer tonight, then fly out the next morning. Valko promised to send them home in good cheer, which probably meant there would be a lot of celebratory drinking at tonight's dinner. What better way to cement the new relationship between allies?

THE DINNER WAS AS INFORMAL AS A DINNER CAN BE WHEN it's given in the Bulgarian president's home. The president was an eloquent man who'd risen first through the ranks of the army, then through the echelons of politics to attain his current post.

Cal learned that the president had been Valko's sergeant when the gruff Bulgarian had first enlisted. Cal couldn't help but laugh as the politician told them stories about young Private Valko's first days of service to the motherland. Luckily

Valko laughed along with them, the endless supply of Bulgarian booze no doubt helping.

By the time dessert was served, everyone but Daniel had had their fair share of drinks and food. One of the president's ministers was snoring loudly in the corner, and another looked like he was about to fall out of his chair. Cal wasn't drunk, but he was sure he couldn't put another bite in his mouth. He was stuffed.

"Which way's the bathroom?" he asked Valko.

The Bulgarian pointed to an ornately carved wooden door in the corner.

"Do not fall in," said a visibly inebriated Valko.

Cal chuckled and slid back from the table. Maybe a little walk would make room for dessert.

* * *

THE GUARD CHECKED THE VISITOR'S IDENTIFICATION again. Something seemed familiar, like deja vu. Hadn't this man already come into the presidential compound? Maybe he'd left while the guard was on break and was now returning. He checked the visitor's list and there was the name.

He handed the military identification back to the impatient man sitting in the idling Mercedes Benz. Supposedly he was a friend of the president. It said so on the list, and the list had never been wrong.

He shrugged off the unease as the man drove into the complex and found a parking spot in the third row.

* * *

DANIEL WATCHED THE REVELRY WITH SILENT AMUSEMENT. It was good to see Valko letting off some steam. The Marine knew what it was like to have so much pent up anger simmering inside. For years he'd battled his own demons after leaving the Marine Corps. He understood Valko's torment, and hoped this was a sign of things to come.

The sniper glanced at his watch. Almost midnight. While he didn't mind the late hour, he'd hoped to get a couple hours of sleep before morning. By the looks of the men around the expansive table, the festivities were just getting revved up.

Daniel smiled and took another sip of his water.

* * *

BULGARIA'S MINISTER OF FOREIGN AFFAIRS TRIED TO focus on putting one foot in front of the other. His wife would not be happy that a) he was coming home so late, and b) he was so drunk. It didn't happen often, but his wife, a strict religious type, always gave him the cold shoulder when he arrived home in such a state. *No sex tonight*, he thought. Unlike the majority of his colleagues, he found his wife extremely alluring. Maybe it was because, in direct contrast to her pious public lifestyle, she was a lioness in the bedroom.

As he neared the stairs leading down to the foyer, the minister heard footsteps coming up. His vision blurry, it took a moment for his eyes to focus. *I must be seeing things*, he thought, chiding himself for drinking too much.

He raised a hand and smiled. "Valko, didn't I just leave you in the dining room?" the minister asked, his words slurring.

The man didn't answer, just kept coming closer. The minister tried once again to focus by shaking his head. When he opened his eyes, the man who looked like Stojan Valko was pointing a long pistol at his head. Rather than be alarmed, the minister's face scrunched in confusion. He'd known Stojan since taking office three years before. The Special Forces soldier was a personal friend of the president. Maybe he was drunk too and playing a prank. The minister giggled.

"Stojan, why are you—"

The two silenced blasts from the Makarov pistol quieted the minister forever. Stepping over the dead foreign minister, Valko's twin walked toward the dining room.

* * *

CAL CHECKED HIS EMAIL AFTER WASHING HIS HANDS IN THE expansively luxurious bathroom. He was sure the first house he remembered living in when his dad was stationed at Camp Lejeune could've fit in there. Why did someone need that many benches and sinks in a private bathroom?

Cal skimmed the messages and smiled at the sound of renewed laugher from the dining room. *I better start drinking water*, he thought as he deleted a message from Neil and then opened one from Diane. They'd kept in regular contact despite his hectic schedule. It was odd to be on the battle-field and still have the ability to connect back home. The luxury was something old veterans never had in Korea, Vietnam or even the First Gulf War.

He read the short note from Diane, imagining how her face might've crinkled as she wrote it.

Cal, I'm sorry I missed your call this morning. It's been crazy around here. I can't wait to see you when you get back. This time dinner's on me. Let me know when you can talk on the phone.
- Diane

HE REREAD THE NOTE AND THEN TAPPED ON THE REPLY

icon. Just as he went to type his response, he heard a commotion from the dining room. It sounded like someone had knocked a plate or a platter off the table.

Cal went to the door and reached for the handle.

* * *

IT WAS EASIER THAN HE'D THOUGHT. THERE WASN'T MUCH that money couldn't buy. A new suit. A fresh haircut and shave. A duplicate military identification card.

Kiril Valko had found out about his brother's involvement in Iraq soon after the elder Valko fled to Syria. While jets flew overhead and bombs rattled the ground, Kiril found his brother.

He'd kept periodic tabs on his twin brother. For example, he'd known that Stojan was a Special Forces soldier and that he'd served with the current Bulgarian president. Kiril didn't know the extent of his brother's military experience, but he'd found everything he needed once the millions were spent.

The man who'd become The Master had always kept distant contacts within his mother country. There were Islamic sympathizers in almost every government around the world, and currency could always be counted on to loosen their atrophied tongues. If money didn't work, threats always did.

So he'd connected with an old friend from his time in jail who now worked as a private cook for the Bulgarian National Assembly. Then there were the guards he'd bribed and the assistants he'd blackmailed. Luckily, the president of Bulgaria was inferior to its prime minister, and this allowed easier access for the leader of ISIS. Years of practice honed his craft. Getting to his target was child's play for the master tactician. Besides, he had a secret weapon.

Kiril didn't hesitate when he slipped into the room,

shooting three of the six men sitting with their backs turned. They fell to the floor, taking stem wear and platters with them.

Those left saw what he held. In his right hand was the pistol. In his left was a trigger, a thin blue wire running from his half unbuttoned shirt where a vest of explosives was strapped to his chest.

The president stared in his drunk stupor much like the minister he'd killed on the landing. His brother glared at him from across the table, the veins in his neck bulging. There was a third. A man with a calm face and snake-like eyes, whose blond hair was tied back in a ponytail. Kiril didn't know who he was. It didn't matter.

"Come with me, brother," said Kiril, grinning at Stojan.

"The guards?" asked Stojan.

"Dead," lied Kiril. "Come. If we go now, your president may live."

His brother wasn't stupid. He might not be as smart as him, but the Bulgarian warrior could see that his older twin meant what he'd said. Besides, the men squirming on the floor had limited time. They would die if they weren't given medical attention soon.

Stojan rose from his chair, slowly making his way around the disheveled table.

"What do you want?" asked Stojan.

"You will see," replied Kiril.

* * *

CAL LISTENED FROM THE DOOR. HE COULDN'T UNDERSTAND what either of the men was saying, but he saw the trigger in the man's hand through the cracked bathroom door. Cal couldn't see the man's face, and figured the stranger was some nut job who wanted to kill the president. That was just their luck. Come to Bulgaria for dinner and end up in a life or death confrontation.

Cal quickly examined his options. If the explosive were rigged with a dead man's switch, he surely had enough to level half the building. That meant Cal couldn't shoot the guy without risking his life and the lives of the six men in the room.

He bet Daniel was thinking the same thing, and that was why the sniper hadn't moved. Without another alternative, Cal watched as Stojan Valko approached the intruder.

PRIVATE HOME OF THE PRESIDENT OF BULGARIA

12:03AM, AUGUST 19TH

K iril kept his pistol trained on his brother, his opposite hand maintaining pressure on the dead man's switch. He'd set the sensitivity level himself, ensuring a detonation should he be disabled by an attacker.

He watched his brother come closer, tried to read his face. As children, they'd often stayed up late trying to read each other's minds. He'd once read a scientific report that said twins, especially identical twins, had certain intertwined abilities that science didn't completely understand.

Kiril had not only spent his years away becoming a deadly terrorist, but he'd read anything he could put his hands on about twins. It was a passion he'd never given up, and never told anyone about.

So as his brother inched closer, he tried again to read his brother's thoughts, to feel his emotions. He'd always wished that someday they'd be reunited and find a common cause to fight for, to die for. He dared to believe. Maybe this was the day.

* * *

A WHIRLWIND OF EMOTIONS SWEPT THROUGH STOJAN AS HE approached his brother. Images of his mother and father sneaked from the depths of his memories and into his subconscious. He remembered the anger he felt toward his father, the pain caused by his death. He remembered the despair of his mother and how she'd withered away until death finally took her.

Above it all, he remembered the closeness he'd always felt with his brother. Even when he'd seen him last, banishing Kiril from his sight, he'd felt like his heart had been ripped out as his brother left through the door.

Every raw emotion and moment of bitter angst came screaming back. He was a child again, yearning for the love of his brother, wanting to be one.

His eyes pleaded as six feet, and then five feet sat before them.

* * *

KIRIL SAW THE CHANGE IN STOJAN'S EYES. HE SUDDENLY felt the familiar feeling of having his brother close. The years had not changed a thing. They were one. The thought gave him hope.

"Come, brother," he beckoned.

He saw tears in Stojan's eyes. Tears! This was his brother, the tough warrior, the son who'd wanted to be like their father, the one with no emotion. Surely this was a sign. This was Allah granting him a gift amidst his loss, the death of thousands of his loyal brothers only to regain his true brother.

Tears came to his own eyes as Stojan spread his arms. The two brothers embraced.

* * *

Cal watched in shock as Stojan Valko hugged the man who was wrapped in explosives. Then he understood. This was the brother. The Master. The murderer.

Regret and anger flooded Cal's chest. His mind seethed. How could he have been so stupid, so naive? *He's been in on it all along.*

Cal gripped the pistol in his hand, and waited for the right moment to kill the two together. Maybe he'd get lucky and the explosives wouldn't go off. But then maybe they would and he'd be screwed for good.

He didn't care.

* * *

The flood of feeling was like a torrent, filling Kiril's heart. This was what he'd always wanted. He'd killed his own father for his brother. He'd left to build a new world, a world for twins bonded for all time. Deep down he knew why, but he'd never admitted it until now.

He loved his brother despite their disagreements, despite their time apart. Kiril was whole. He wondered if it had all been about the journey, some adventure crafted by Allah simply for the union of two brothers.

All was right. All was good. *Allahu akbar,* he thought. God is good.

* * *

Cal eased the door open. Neither brother seemed to notice until he stepped one foot out. Stojan's eyes snapped open and they met Cal's glare.

Stojan blinked, but didn't move and he didn't say anything

to his brother. Then, just perceptibly, Stojan nodded to Cal and made his move.

* * *

KIRIL FELT HIS BROTHER RELEASE THEIR EMBRACE UNTIL they stared at each other, faces inches apart. They looked so much alike, true identical twins. One the mirror reflection of the other.

"I love you, brother," said Stojan, the words filling Kiril's heart to bursting.

"I—"

Kiril's eyes widened as Stojan's hands snapped out and grasped both of his own.

"What are you doing?" Kiril growled.

"What I should have done long ago," Stojan said evenly, his strength far surpassing Kiril's.

The pistol clattered to the floor, and suddenly Kiril was moving, not by his own power, but carried by his powerful younger brother.

* * *

CAL UNDERSTOOD WHAT VALKO WAS DOING AND BURST from the room just as the grappling brothers moved. His legs felt like cement blocks as time slowed. He saw Daniel flipping the thick dining room table over.

Cal dove at the stunned president, tackling him to the ground. They landed behind the overturned table, just as the Valko brothers crashed through the huge glass window on the opposite side of the large room and fell down the three stories to the cobblestone courtyard below.

The seconds sludged by, no sound, no explosion, and then there was only darkness.

THE WHITE HOUSE

President Zimmer stared out the Oval Office window, willing the words to come. He'd already crumpled three pieces of his personal stationary. Nothing seemed to be enough.

Letters of condolence weren't the easiest thing to write, but usually the words came. Today they wouldn't. He didn't know what to say.

The ringing from his intercom startled him.

"Yes?"

"Mr. President, your 10:30 is here. You wanted me to tell you if they got here early," said the president's secretary, a hint of annoyance in her tone. The swarthy old gatekeeper liked precise timekeeping. When anything, even an early appearance, popped up, she let everyone know her displeasure.

"Send them in, please."

Zimmer stood from his work and walked toward the door as his guests stepped in.

Cal Stokes had his right arm in a sling and a stitched gash over his left eye. Daniel Briggs walked in behind his boss, looking no worse for wear.

"Look at what the cat dragged in," said Zimmer, hoping he'd read Cal's mood correctly. He couldn't tell what the Marine was thinking, a rare event for the warrior who usually wore his emotions like campaign buttons.

Thankfully, Cal grinned.

"You must be talking about me because once again Ol' Snake Eyes escaped the clutches of doom unscathed."

Zimmer chuckled and shook his friends' hands. He was happy to see them, but was concerned about why Cal had requested the meeting. There'd been something in his tone when he called after the thing in Bulgaria that the president couldn't read.

Once they were all settled on the couches, the president asked, "What did you want to see me about?"

"The Bulgarian president is giving Stojan Valko some kind of national medal, posthumously. I think we should do the same."

"Okay. I don't see why that should be a problem."

Zimmer waited for Cal to continue.

"I need to ask you a question," said Cal evenly.

"Shoot."

"All that stuff you said on television, everything they're saying on the news about *The Zimmer Doctrine*. I need to know that you meant it."

Zimmer resisted the urge to argue. As a first-term congressman, he would have. He'd always been one to blow up when his feathers got ruffled. The tantrum of a petulant child.

But things were different now. Too many lessons to count. Humbled. Broken down and built back up. He was a politician who'd been given a second chance, who'd seen the truth behind the murk of politics. And no one had helped more than the man sitting in front of him, the man who was now questioning his resolve.

"You know I meant it, Cal."

"I know you did at the time, in the moment. But what happens in a year, in three years, when you're trying to get re-elected and scumbags are trying to make you look like a war-monger?"

It was a fair question. The sands of the political arena shifted as readily as a feather in the wind. Unguided. Aimless. Lost.

"All I can say is that I'm in for the long haul. You and your team did the hard part, the stuff I could never do. For that I am eternally thankful. But this is my turf, my fight. If they want to come at me, I'll come back swinging. You taught me that. Fight for what you believe in, right?"

Cal stared at the president, a look of amusement in his eyes.

"I guess you *can* teach a spoiled democrat new tricks," said Cal.

The president shrugged. "As long as I'm surrounded by jarheads like you."

* * *

CAMP CAVALIER - CHARLOTTESVILLE, VIRGINIA - 5:58PM

They'd come without being asked. They saw it as their duty. A tribute to a fallen comrade.

There was only silence as the blood red sun sunk into the horizon. They stood in a half-circle, facing the sunset, saying their last goodbyes.

Daniel Briggs stood to Cal's left and MSgt Trent and Gaucho to his right. The foreigners filled in the rest; the Brits led by one-eyed Kreyling, the Australians by the youthful Fox, the Japanese by the skilled Kokubu, and the Italians by the gregarious Moretti. They'd met as strangers, but now gathered as family.

The Bulgarians were home burying their comrade, their president presiding over a national memorial the next day.

Cal had learned long ago that warriors have perhaps the keenest sense of the word *family*. To those who fight, not knowing whether death lies waiting around the next bend, family is the only tangible thing they know. Many embrace their own version of God or say they do it for king and country, but when it all comes to a head, they believe in the man standing next to them. *Family*.

So while their relationships were still young, their lives were forever bound. No man would hesitate to come to the aid of the other. They were family now, a fact that made Cal prouder than the victories they'd reaped in battle.

After all, for men such as these, war was just a game, a deadly game with high stakes, but a game nonetheless. But family... now that was something to fight for, something to live for, something to cherish.

EPILOGUE

Cal and Diane walked along the pathways of the University of Virginia as if in a trance. Neither one knew where they were going, too consumed were they with each other.

Cal's dislocated shoulder was healing and his eye wasn't as swollen as before. Diane had been concerned, had asked how he'd been hurt. Cal lied, telling her that he'd been in a car accident. He knew by the look in her eyes that she saw right through him. She knew he was lying. But he couldn't tell her. He barely knew her. And besides, what he did for a living was completely off limits as far as a topic of conversation.

He had to keep up the illusion that he was a normal guy, someone who punched the clock and pulled in a regular paycheck. Cal told himself she would never understand.

For her part, Diane didn't press. She seemed genuinely happy they were together. To Cal it felt like things were complete. He'd not only found his calling, but he might've found the missing piece, the woman who might help mend his broken heart. Her skin pressed against his as they walked hand-in-hand down the brick-paved pathways of Mr. Jefferson's university.

By the time they got back to Diane's apartment, they were ready for dinner. They'd walked for hours. Sometimes they talked, but mostly they just enjoyed each other's company. Cal liked that he felt as comfortable with her in silence as he did in discussing the latest Washington Redskins news. There was a connection there he couldn't explain.

While Diane took a shower, Cal clicked on the television and channel surfed until he found some mildly amusing reality TV show. He couldn't take the news, never had, but something about reality TV always seemed to pull him in.

Just as Cal chuckled when some orthopedic surgeon chewed out her porn-loving husband, his phone rang. There was no number and he was tempted to let it go to voicemail. The shower was still running, so he shrugged and answered the phone.

"Hello?"

There was no voice, just a crackling sound in the background.

"Hello?" Cal asked again.

"Cal," came the whispered voice.

"Who is this?" Cal asked, sitting up straighter.

"It's Andy."

"Hey, man, where are you?" The last thing Cal had heard was that his friend, Marine Corps Major Andrews, was in the Middle East.

"I don't have much time. They know I'm here and—"

More crackling in the background. Suddenly Cal realized what it was. *Gunfire*.

"Andy, what—"

"Listen. Get a hold of Rich Isnard. He'll know—"

There was shouting in Arabic and more gunfire. Then the line went dead.

* * *

I hope you enjoyed this story.
If you did, please take a moment to write a review <u>ON AMAZON</u>. Even the short ones help!

GET A FREE COPY OF THE CORPS JUSTICE PREQUEL SHORT STORY, *GOD-SPEED*, JUST FOR SUBSCRIBING AT <u>CG-COOPER.COM</u>

ALSO BY C. G. COOPER

ABOUT THE AUTHOR

C. G. Cooper is the *USA TODAY* and AMAZON BESTSELLING author of the CORPS JUSTICE novels (including spinoffs), The Chronicles of Benjamin Dragon and the Patriot Protocol series.

Cooper grew up in a Navy family and traveled from one Naval base to another as he fed his love of books and a fledgling desire to write.

Upon graduating from the University of Virginia with a degree in Foreign Affairs, Cooper was commissioned in the United States Marine Corps and went on to serve six years as an infantry officer. C. G. Cooper's final Marine duty station was in Nashville, Tennessee, where he fell in love with the laid-back lifestyle of Music City.

His first published novel, BACK TO WAR, came out of a need to link back to his time in the Marine Corps. That novel, written as a side project, spawned many follow-on novels, several exciting spinoffs, and catapulted Cooper's career.

Cooper lives just south of Nashville with his wife, three children, and their German shorthaired pointer, Liberty, who's become a popular character in the Corps Justice novels.

When he's not writing or hosting his podcast, Books In 30, Cooper spends time with his family, does his best to improve his golf handicap, and loves to shed light on the ongoing fight of everyday heroes.

Cooper loves hearing from readers and responds to every email personally.
To connect with C. G. Cooper visit
www.cg-cooper.com

64861724R00131

Made in the USA
Columbia, SC
12 July 2019